HOWDY!

Welcome to the Circle C. My name is Andi Carter. If you are a new reader, here's a quick roundup of my family, friends, and adventures:

I'm a tomboy who lives on a huge cattle ranch near Fresno, California, in the exciting 1880s. I would rather ride my palomino mare, Taffy, than do anything else. I mean well, but trouble just seems to follow me around.

Our family includes my mother, Elizabeth, my ladylike older sister, Melinda, and my three older brothers: Justin (a lawyer), Chad, and Mitch. I love them, but sometimes they treat me like a pest. My father was killed in a ranch accident a few years ago.

In **Long Ride Home**, Taffy is stolen and it's my fault. I set out to find my horse and end up far from home and in a heap of trouble.

In **Dangerous Decision**, I nearly trample my new teacher in a horse race with my friend Cory. Later, I have to make a life-or-death choice.

Next, I discover I'm the only one who doesn't know the Carter **Family Secret**, and it turns my world upside down.

In **San Francisco Smugglers**, a flood sends me to school in the city for two months. My new roommate, Jenny, and I discover that the little Chinese servant-girl in our school is really a slave.

Trouble with Treasure is what Jenny, Cory, and I find when we head into the mountains with Mitch to pan for gold.

And now I may lose my beloved horse, Taffy, if I tell what I saw in **Price of Truth**.

So saddle up and ride into my latest adventure!

Andi

ANDREA CARTER AND THE

Long Ride Home

THE CIRCLE C ADVENTURES SERIES

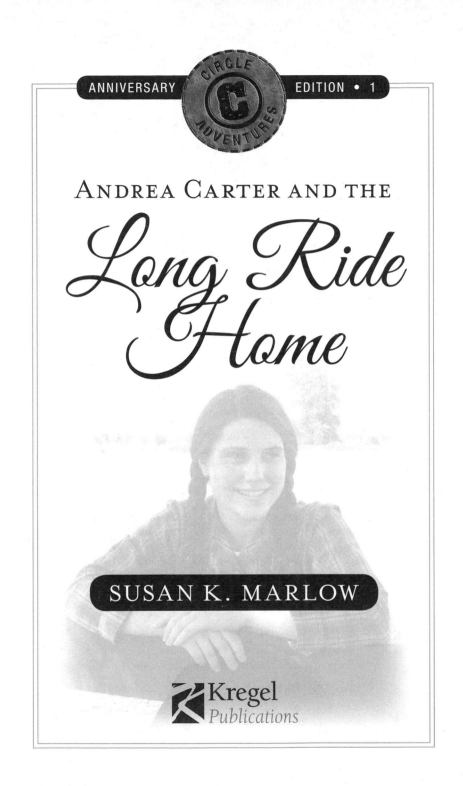

ANNIVERSARY · EDITION · 1

CIRCLE C ADVENTURES

ANDREA CARTER AND THE

Long Ride Home

SUSAN K. MARLOW

Kregel
Publications

Printed in the United States of America
16 17 18 19 20 21 22 23 24 25 / 5 4 3 2 1

1044138

CONTENTS

Chapter One

IT'S NOT FAIR!

"It's Saturday at last!" Andi Carter leaped from her bed and threw open the doors that led onto the balcony of her family's two-story ranch house. She hurried out into the early morning, leaned far over the railing, and breathed in the fresh new California day.

"This is going to be a great day," Andi announced, tossing her unruly mass of long, dark hair behind her shoulder. She could not hide her joy at the thought of a whole day to ride her horse, Taffy, and do as she liked.

She leaned farther over the railing, hoping to catch a glimpse of her brother Chad's new stallion. The corral next to the barn was just beyond sight, but if she climbed over the railing and balanced on the narrow overhang, she might be able to see the magnificent animal— if only for a moment.

Putting thoughts into action, Andi scurried over the railing, hampered only slightly by her long, white nightgown. She could almost hear her mother's disapproving voice. *"Really, Andrea. Proper young ladies do* not *climb balconies in their nightgowns!"* She smiled at the thought and shaded her eyes against the rising sun.

Before Andi could get a good view of the horse, the sun cleared the distant peaks of the Sierra Nevada, and she was forced to narrow her eyes against the brightness that erupted around her. The ranch house, styled after the lovely and practical Spanish *haciendas* of an earlier age, burst into dazzling white against the bright blue sky.

"I can't see a thing," she muttered, disappointed.

"*Buenos días, señorita,*" a cheerful voice hailed her from below. "What are you doing?"

Andi whirled, slipped, and nearly lost her balance. She reached out to steady herself against the railing and looked down. Diego, one of the hired hands, stood leaning against a rake, grinning up at her.

"I . . . well . . . I was trying to see Chad's new stallion," came Andi's embarrassed reply. She scrambled back over the railing and onto the safety of the balcony.

Diego glanced in the direction of the corral, then up at Andi. He shook his head. "Why do you not go and look at the horse from nearer the corral, like everyone else?"

Andi had no answer for the Mexican ranch hand. She felt herself turning red and hoped with all her heart that Diego would keep this encounter to himself. Without a word, she spun around and re-entered her bedroom, closing the doors with a bang.

"What a way to start the day." But Andi couldn't help breaking into a grin at how she must have looked, hanging onto the balcony and wearing only her nightgown. No doubt Diego was having a good laugh over it while he tended the gardens.

She hurried across her room and began to dress, pulling on her favorite pair of faded overalls and a gingham shirt. How glad she was that Mother didn't always force her to wear what other young ladies going on twelve had to wear—dresses and tiny slippers and other uncomfortable trappings. On Saturdays, Andi was allowed to wear what she pleased, so long as she didn't step foot off the ranch.

"After all," Andi declared, pulling on one of her riding boots, "this *is* 1880. There are a lot of new ideas about what a girl can wear."

A door slammed. Andi paused in her dressing and listened. Only Chad slammed doors like that, and then only when he was upset about something.

"Andi! Get down here!" Chad's voice traveled up the stairs and through her bedroom door like the sound of a gunshot.

Andi winced. *Oh, no. What have I done wrong this time?* She quickly pulled on the other boot and made her way to the vanity. Pouring a tiny amount of water from the milk-white pitcher into the washbasin, she splashed the cold liquid on her face.

A small knot of worry began to form in Andi's stomach as she hastily braided her thick, dark hair into two long plaits. What could have upset Chad first thing in the morning?

Andi gave a quick glance around her less-than-spotless room and frowned. She really should take time to straighten it, but if she didn't find out what Chad wanted, he'd start yelling again. "I'll clean it later," she decided, half hoping that Luisa, their housekeeper, might look in on her room and spare a few minutes to clean it for her.

Andi made her way from her room but stopped at the top of the stairs. Reaching out her hand, she ran it along the smooth surface of the banister. *Just this once,* she persuaded herself.

Determined not to let Chad ruin her morning, she settled herself onto the railing. Lifting her feet, she sailed down the banister and landed on the foyer floor with a loud *thump*. She grinned and picked herself up from the floor. Sliding down the banister was such fun!

So long as Luisa doesn't catch me.

Her cheerful mood instantly restored, Andi entered the dining room with a spring in her step. She greeted her mother and older sister, who were finishing their breakfast in companionable silence.

"Good morning, Andrea," Mother replied with a smile. "Luisa just brought in a fresh plate of hotcakes. Sit down and have some before they get cold."

Andi sat down in the empty seat next to her sister and pretended not to notice that seventeen-year-old Melinda hadn't returned the greeting. Andi shrugged it off and helped herself to a stack of still-warm pancakes, smothering them in butter and maple syrup.

She's probably mad at me, Andi concluded. *Somebody's always upset with me these days.*

"Chad's looking for you," Melinda announced.

"I know," Andi said uneasily. "I heard him. The whole ranch can hear him when he yells."

Mother wrinkled her forehead. "I wonder what upset him this early in the day."

Andi didn't know, but she was certain it wouldn't be long before she found out. Her cheerful mood began to dissolve.

"So, here you are."

Andi looked up. Her twenty-six-year-old brother stood just inside the doorway. It was easy to see he was irritated about something. He wasn't smiling, and his blue eyes were stormy. He lifted a finger and pointed it at Andi. "I'd like a word with you."

"What about?" Andi speared a forkful of pancake and swirled it around in the syrup. She hoped Chad wasn't in one of his bossy moods. Just because he was in charge of running the ranch didn't mean he could tell her what to do all the time.

"I've just come from the barn," Chad said, "where I discovered about a dozen thirsty horses, yours included."

Oh, no! Andi sprang from her chair in sudden panic. Her eyes widened at the awful realization that she had neglected her chores. "I'm sorry. I forgot. I'll do it right away." She hurried around the table but didn't get far.

Chad held out his arm to prevent her leaving. "Never mind. Mitch is taking care of it." He shook his head. "You were supposed to do it yesterday after school."

"I know, but . . ." Her voice faltered. "Some of the men were breaking those new broncos out in the north corral. They said I could watch for a few minutes. I was going to check the horses after supper, but—". She broke off and ducked her head. "I'm sorry."

"You're *always* sorry," Chad said with an impatient sigh. He folded his arms across his chest and looked down at his sister. He nodded at her overalls and boots. "I'm glad to see you're dressed for work today. You're going to muck out every stall in the horse barn."

Andi's head snapped up. "Muck out the *stalls*? That's the ranch hands' job, not mine."

"Today it's your job."

"It'll take all day!"

"Good. It'll keep you out of trouble."

"Mother!" Andi turned to her mother in a desperate appeal. "Please don't make me clean stalls today. It's my only free day. I want to go riding."

Elizabeth Carter's soft blue eyes were full of understanding, but her voice was firm. "I'm sorry, Andrea. This is the third time in two weeks Chad has had to remind you about those horses. Checking their water is not a difficult task. Perhaps cleaning out stalls will help your memory."

Andi opened her mouth to protest. Then she closed it. Her mother was not going to budge. Ever since her father's death in an accident during spring roundup six years ago, her mother had turned over the running of the Circle C ranch to Andi's three older brothers. She rarely went against any decision Chad made regarding the day-to-day management of the ranch.

"Better get started." Chad poured himself a cup of coffee and joined his mother and Melinda at the table.

"It's not fair," Andi grumbled, reaching across the table for some sugar cubes for her horse. "One little mistake." She pocketed the sugar and turned toward the door. "My whole day is ruined."

"It's your own fault," Chad called after her.

Andi left the house in a huff. She kicked the dust and made her way toward the huge barn that stabled some of the finest horses in the San Joaquin Valley. Though most of the working horses were kept outdoors in a large corral, to be lassoed each day for work, there were always a few stabled in the barn. It was Andi's job to feed and water them.

She reached the barn and leaned against the wide double doors before entering. "Oh, Justin, I wish you were home. I'm hardly ever in trouble when you're around." She sighed. Her oldest and favorite brother had gone to Sacramento—again. Why couldn't he stay home and help Chad and Mitch run the ranch, instead of running off to San Francisco or Sacramento every few months?

"I'm sure Governor Perkins can run California without your help," she muttered. It was an old story. Justin was often away—doing whatever it was lawyers do—and no amount of wishing would bring him home any sooner.

With a sudden, urgent desire to get the miserable stall-cleaning job done, Andi pushed Justin from her thoughts. She shoved the heavy barn doors open and slipped inside, adjusting her eyes to the dim interior. The familiar odors of dusty hay, horses, and old leather greeted her.

She paused to enjoy the sweet scent of last summer's alfalfa then picked up a pitchfork, found the wheelbarrow, and made her way to her horse's stall. The palomino mare whinnied with eagerness at the sight of her young mistress. She thrust her golden head over the stall's half-door and nipped playfully at Andi's shoulder. *Let me out of here!* she seemed to be saying.

"You hate being cooped up, don't you, Taffy? I reckon your paddock out back isn't roomy enough for a good romp. Sorry, I'm just being selfish. You stay so much cleaner indoors."

Andi unlatched the stall's door and entered, patting Taffy in apology. "Listen, girl. Your troubles are nothing compared to mine." She began to clean the stall and unload her complaints onto her best friend, the one companion who always listened patiently. "I don't know what's wrong, but I can't seem to do anything right these days."

She stopped and leaned on the pitchfork. "How could I have been so stupid as to leave that open jar of spiders in Melinda's room last week?" She lunged at a pile of soiled straw bedding and tossed it through the open doorway. The load missed the wheelbarrow and landed in the middle of the walkway.

14

Andi sighed and went after the mess. "Nobody believed me when I said it was an accident. I only wanted to see the new stallion Chad and Mitch were bringing home. Everybody knows Melinda's room has the best view of the corral. I didn't mean to forget about the spiders."

She returned to the stall. "Really, Taffy, I didn't. Everything just happened so fast when the stallion broke out. Two of the men almost got trampled, and Jake Barnes got his arm broke!"

Andi gave Taffy a shove to encourage her to move over. "You should have seen Melinda at breakfast the next morning. She slammed the empty jar down right in front of me. When I saw those red bites all over her face and arms, I knew I was in trouble. Guess what I did the rest of the morning?" She walked around to face her horse. "Are you listening to me?"

Taffy stamped an impatient foot. Andi took it as a sign that she should continue her tale. "I spent the entire morning searching for and killing spiders. Then Mother made me scrub every crack in Melinda's floor and wash down the walls. I've decided not to collect spiders anymore."

She shuddered, remembering her sister's mood at breakfast. "At least not until Melinda cools down. I think she's still mad at me."

Andi leaned the pitchfork against the wall and turned back to her horse, giving the mare an affectionate pat. Taffy snorted and tossed her head, as if eager to hear more.

Andi was happy to oblige. "If spiders aren't bad enough, listen to what happened in school last week." She grabbed a brush and started grooming the palomino's coat. "Remember that big frog I found near the creek a couple of weeks ago? I took it to school."

Taffy snorted and laid her ears back.

"Yeah, it wasn't one of my better ideas. But Cory and I had a deal. He was going to swap me five aggies for the frog. Before we could make the trade at recess, though, Miss Hall found the frog in my desk." She cringed at the memory. "She scolded me in front of the

15

entire class and sent me to the corner. The *corner*, Taffy! I was in disgrace the rest of the day." Andi sighed. "Now, I've got no frog and no marbles."

She tossed the brush into a corner and picked up the pitchfork again. Spiders, frogs, forgetting her chores, leaving her room a mess—the list went on and on. She shook her head. Absolutely nothing had gone right since Justin left for Sacramento, and here she was on her only free day—stuck in the barn.

A sudden, distinctive whinny pulled Andi from another spell of daydreaming. She finished up Taffy's stall and leaned the pitchfork against one of the large posts that supported the loft above. The whinny came again, a call from the corral next to the barn.

Andi peeked through the open barn doors and into the corral. A rush of longing filled her heart. There he was—Chad's new black stallion. Prince Loco stood well over sixteen hands high, with a temper to match his size. He was the most beautiful horse Andi had ever seen. And the most dangerous.

From the moment the stallion had arrived on the ranch, Andi had begged to help with the gentling. Horses trusted her, she insisted. There wasn't a horse on the entire ranch she couldn't ride.

All her pleading had amounted to nothing. She was allowed to watch Chad work with Prince Loco—from a safe distance—but told never to go near him alone.

Chad was the ranch boss. His word was law, and Mother backed him up every time.

"It's not fair." Andi watched the magnificent horse run along the corral fence. "Chad treats me like I'm too little to do anything. If only he would give me a chance. I'd show him that horse would like me."

She leaned against the doorpost and shoved her hands into her pockets, ignoring her chores and gazing at the gorgeous black animal. She felt the small, hard lumps at the bottom of her pocket and remembered Taffy had not yet been given her weekly treat of sugar.

With a sigh, Andi pulled the sugar from her pocket and turned toward Taffy's stall. *I'd better get back to those stalls before Chad catches me loafing.*

Then she paused. A flickering of an idea tickled the back of her mind. She uncurled her fingers and stared at the white lumps lying in her palm. Her heart fluttered. *I know I can do it,* she decided suddenly. She pushed aside the thought of whether she *should* do it.

Andi raised her head and looked over at the stallion. *I'm old enough to do this. I'll prove to Chad his stallion isn't as wild as he thinks.* She took a step away from the barn and into the yard.

Chapter Two

A Close Call

A ndi stopped and gave a low whistle, the same greeting Chad always used to announce his presence around the horse. She waited, holding her breath.

Prince Loco stopped short. He pricked up his ears and turned his head in her direction. With that sign of encouragement, Andi relaxed. She made her way slowly and quietly toward the corral, whistling softly.

The stallion shied away to the other side of the corral when Andi approached. He paced back and forth and stamped the ground. He seemed to recognize the whistle but not the whistler. He laid his ears back in warning.

Andi hesitated. She glanced around the yard for signs of life. She definitely didn't want an audience.

The yard was deserted.

Little by little, Andi hoisted herself to the top railing of the corral and sat quietly, watching the stallion. *So far, so good.* Prince Loco regarded her for an instant and then moved a few paces closer. Was his curiosity getting the better of him?

"C'mon, you beautiful thing," Andi urged in a low whisper. "You know I'd never hurt you, don't you? Listen. I whistle just like Chad." She whistled softly and waited.

Andi knew patience was the key to gentling any horse. Hadn't

Chad taught her that when they'd trained Taffy together all those years ago? It was time to show her brother she remembered the lesson. Andi would wait as long as it took for the stallion to realize she was not a threat.

Prince Loco snorted. He shook his head then advanced a few steps.

Andi's heart skipped. She glanced into her open hand. The sugar was beginning to melt. She took a deep breath and extended her palm. "See here, Loco. I've got you one special treat. I brought it out for Taffy, but if you come over here and show me you can behave, I'll let you have it." She kept her voice calm, gentle, and convincing.

The stallion looked interested. He took a few more steps then whinnied and trotted away. He stopped at the far end of the corral and regarded Andi with wild eyes.

Andi whistled again. *Patience.* She was prepared to stay on top of the fence the rest of the morning to convince that horse to do one thing: eat sugar from her hand.

Chad will surely let me help out when he sees his wild stallion taking sugar from me. The thought made her smile. She held out her hand a little farther. "C'mon, fella."

Prince Loco pranced and tossed his head, then he suddenly rose up on his hind legs.

Andi caught her breath. The stallion was so magnificent she could scarcely breathe. Powerful muscles flexed under his shimmering black coat. He advanced to within a few arm-lengths and came down on all fours, snorting his uneasiness and curiosity.

Andi's eyes grew wide at his nearness. She tightened her grip on the fence and bit her lip in sudden indecision. Maybe this was not such a good idea. Loco looked huge up close.

She swallowed her uncertainty. *I can do this.* She extended her hand as far as she could without tumbling into the corral. "Come and get it," she crooned.

The horse took a step.

"That's right, boy. One more step and it's yours." Andi wanted nothing more than to touch his velvet nose. *But I won't touch him. Not this first time.* She would sit perfectly still and let Loco learn to trust her.

The stallion shook his mane, settled down, and nibbled at the sugar in Andi's outstretched palm.

Her heart swelled with joy. "I knew you and I could be friends. Just wait 'til Chad—"

Without warning, the enormous animal reared up and whinnied a challenge. The blood drained from Andi's face. *Jump down!* her mind screamed, but she couldn't move. Her arms and legs were frozen with fear. She choked back a cry and watched in horror as the stallion's huge, black hooves bore down on her. *Please, God. Help me!*

An instant later, Andi found herself flying backward through the air. She landed in the dust with a painful *thud* and heard a tremendous *crack*. The stallion's hooves connected with the corral fence and brought it crashing down.

Andi lay on the ground a few yards away and tried to catch her breath, which came in huge gasps. She was shaking so badly, she couldn't even sit up. She had no idea how she'd managed to escape. Had the stallion kicked her off the fence? If so, surely she would have felt his massive hooves slam into her.

She glanced around the yard, which had suddenly come alive with activity. Ranch hands appeared from nowhere. They scurried around the corral in an attempt to keep the frantic horse contained.

A shadow fell across Andi. She looked up. Chad towered over her, hands on his hips, glaring. She had never seen him so furious. His face was dark with anger, and his eyes were chips of blue ice. He shouted some instructions at the ranch hands then turned all of his attention to his sister.

"What were you *doing*?" he bellowed. As usual, the whole ranch could hear him. "You could have been killed!"

Andi bit back a yelp of pain when Chad jerked her up from the ground. He led her over to the splintered railings. "Look at this. That's

20

where you were sitting not one minute ago. It's ruined. Destroyed. If I hadn't come around the barn and yanked you off that fence when I did, you'd be dead now—trampled by a horse you have no business going near."

Andi swallowed hard and stared at the ruined fence. She heard in Chad's shaking voice not only anger but fear for her safety. She had scared him badly with her disobedience, and she was ashamed.

"I'm sorry," she whispered.

"You're *sorry.*" Chad took a deep breath and removed his hat. He wiped the sweat from his forehead and ran his fingers through his thick, black hair. Then he replaced the hat and shook his head. "You know better than to try a fool thing like this. What's wrong with you lately?"

Andi shrugged. Did Chad truly want an answer? Probably not. He looked too angry to listen, anyway.

"You're supposed to be in the barn doing your chores," he said. "Instead, you're out here causing the worst kind of trouble."

He took Andi by the shoulders and forced her to look at him. "I told you to stay away from this horse. He's dangerous. Have you already forgotten about Jake's arm? Or those other two hands who were nearly trampled?"

Andi shook her head, desperately holding back her tears at Chad's rebuke. She hadn't forgotten. She had simply taken for granted that the horse wouldn't hurt *her.*

How wrong she had been! Andi took a deep breath and turned her attention toward the now quiet stallion. "I only wanted to show you I'm old enough to help with—"

"No." Chad held up his hand to cut her off. "I don't want to hear any excuses. You just showed me you're not old enough to do *anything* with this horse. You'd best get back to your chores before I really lose my temper."

"Chad, *please,*" Andi pleaded. "You're right. I shouldn't have done it. I said I was sorry. I won't do it again. Won't you listen?"

"Not this time." Chad glanced over her head to where the men were making repairs on the fence. A shudder went through him. "And one more thing, little sister." He turned his attention back to Andi, raised a finger, and pointed at the stallion. "If I *ever* catch you near that horse again, I'll tan your backside."

An eerie silence fell over the yard. Several ranch hands paused in their work. The stallion snorted.

Heat exploded in Andi's cheeks. Chad could threaten in private to tan her all he liked—he had never followed through—but to embarrass her in front of the hired hands?

"You'll have to catch me first," she challenged, her shame giving way to fury. "Sometimes I wish you weren't my brother!" She burst into tears and took off running toward the barn.

Mitch, the youngest of Andi's three older brothers, whirled as she passed him. "Andi, wait!"

Andi kept running. She had to get away from all those watching eyes.

Stumbling into Taffy's stall, she wrapped her arms around her mare's neck and sobbed. What a terrible day! Taffy stood still, appearing to somehow understand her mistress's distress. Andi stroked the palomino's neck, sniffed back tears, and hugged her again.

"Andi?"

"Go away." She rubbed her face against her shirt sleeve.

Mitch leaned over the stall's half-door and shoved his hat back. "Those were mighty strong words I heard from you a minute ago."

Andi shrugged. Tears threatened to spill over once more. Of course she didn't really wish Chad wasn't her brother. She loved him. Most days, anyway. Why did she always lose her temper and say things she didn't mean?

She shoved away from Taffy and reached past Mitch for her horse's bridle. With a mighty yank, she pulled it from its hook and began to put it on her horse. Her fingers shook with anger and humiliation. "He shamed me, Mitch. He shamed me in front of the entire ranch."

"Can you blame him?" came Mitch's quiet reply. "You should have seen his face when he saw you near that stallion. He was scared."

Andi glanced up from adjusting Taffy's bridle. "Yeah. Scared I'd ruin his precious horse by giving it a lousy lump of sugar."

"That's not true, and you know it," Mitch snapped. Then he sighed. "It's time you faced the facts, Sis. You had a mighty close call today. What got into your head to go near Loco like that?"

Andi shrugged.

"Well, you need to slow down and think things through a bit. Next time Chad might not be there to pull you out."

Andi gathered up the reins and shoved the stall door open without replying. She knew Mitch was right. It just hurt too much to admit it. She pushed past her brother and led Taffy out of the barn and into the bright morning sunshine. Then she grasped the mare's cream-colored mane and slid onto her bare back.

Once Andi left the yard, she urged Taffy into a gallop. The wind tore against her face and ripped apart her carelessly braided hair. It streamed out behind her like the dark mane of the stallion she had so recently left.

If only Justin was here, Andi wailed silently. *He wouldn't let Chad yell at me. He'd fix everything. He always knows what to say. And he's so good at explaining things to Mother.* She cringed when she imagined her mother's likely reaction to her latest bit of foolishness.

Blinking back tears, Andi turned Taffy toward their favorite spot—a clear, bubbling creek up in the east pasture. Nobody went there this time of year. It was the perfect place to be by herself and gather her thoughts before she returned to muck out those awful stalls.

Chapter Three

LATE FOR SUPPER

A gentle nudge and the smell of sweet grass roused Andi from sleep. She opened her eyes and gazed up at Taffy. Her companion and friend towered over her like a golden giant. Andi yawned and stretched, surrounded by the grass and wildflowers of her own special thinking place. Nearby, the creek bubbled noisily.

Andi brushed a dark strand of hair from her face. With a sigh of contentment, she clasped her hands behind her head and stared up into a sapphire-blue sky. She always felt better when she came up here. In her meadow, the sky looked bluer, the grass greener. Even the snow-capped Sierras seemed closer.

Andi rolled over onto her stomach and propped her chin in her hands. She watched Taffy dip her nose into the creek and take a long, slow drink. The mare lifted her head. Clear, sparkling drops fell from her nose.

Andi grinned. "I think I'll join you." She rolled up her sleeves, cupped her hands, and took a cool drink from the stream. Beneath the surface of the water, a silver shape darted past. "Look at the size of that fish, Taffy!" She sat back. "Wish I'd brought my pole. I could have a string of trout in no time. Wouldn't they taste good for lunch?"

Taffy nickered and nudged Andi as if reminding her mistress why she was here. Andi stood up and threw her arms around her horse. "You're right. I can't fish today. I've got too much work to do."

Her stomach tightened at the memory. "You're my best friend, girl." She buried her face in the sweet smell of Taffy's mane. "You're the only one who understands. Justin used to, but he's never around."

Andi released her hold on Taffy and threw herself down next to the creek. Picking up a rock, she tossed it carelessly into the water. "I sure know how to make everybody mad at me lately, don't I?" She picked up another rock and gave it a toss, enjoying the plunk it made as it hit the water. "It's no fun being the youngest. Everyone's always telling me what to do."

Five rocks later Andi was still trying to put the awful morning out of her mind. It was no use. She couldn't stay here much longer. She had to go back, finish the stalls, and try to apologize to Chad again. *Maybe he's cooled off by now*, she thought with little hope.

"Come on. Let's go home." Andi pulled herself up from her spot next to the creek. Her stomach gave a sudden rumble. *I wonder what's for lunch.* She mounted her horse and turned west toward home.

The brightness of the California sun struck Andi full in the face. She pulled back on the reins, puzzled. "Whoa, Taffy." She shaded her eyes and frowned. "The sun can't be going down already. It should be right overhead."

A sudden gust of cool air blew across Andi's face. She shivered. The sun *was* going down, and fast. "Oh, no!" Andi groaned. She had slept away most of the day. There would be no chance to finish all those stalls before supper. In fact, if she didn't hurry, she would be late for the evening meal.

Trouble, trouble, and more trouble. Being on time for meals was one of Mother's strictest rules. Andi had missed the midday meal. She did not want to go without supper.

A rising tide of panic welled up inside her when she noted the sun's position once more. It would take at least half an hour of serious riding to reach the house. She dug her heels into the mare's sides. "Let's get going."

Taffy galloped obediently toward the setting sun for a few minutes. It wasn't long, however, before the mare slowed to a lope, then to a trot.

Andi patted Taffy's neck. "What's the matter?"

One look at her mare's heaving sides gave Andi the answer. Of course. Taffy must have grazed all day while Andi slept. She knew it was unwise—even dangerous—to push her horse after such a meal.

"I'm sorry, " she apologized. "Go as slow as you like." With a sinking heart, she knew she was going to be late for supper.

Very late.

It was almost fully dark when Andi pulled Taffy to a stop in front of the barn. Jumping down, she grabbed the reins and led her horse into the darkened building. Her conscience stabbed her like a knife when she passed the dirty stalls—one by one—on her way to Taffy's stall. She picked up a brush and was about to give Taffy her rubdown, when a voice startled her.

"I'll do that for you, *señorita*."

"Diego! You scared me half to death."

"I'm sorry." The ranch hand chuckled and raised a lantern. It illuminated his dark, grinning face. "You're very late. You have a lot of explaining to do up at the big house." He held out his hand for the brush.

Andi dropped the brush into his hand. "I know. On top of everything else, Luisa will probably yell at me in Spanish."

Diego's smile widened. "No doubt, *señorita*. My Luisa can think of many things to say when she is upset—things you probably do not wish to hear."

Andi shrugged in resignation. "Listen, I've gotta run." She nodded toward Taffy. "You'll make sure she gets a good rubdown, won't you?"

"*Sí, señorita.*"

Andi waved her thanks and raced from the barn. She dashed around the house to the kitchen entrance and threw open the door. Breathless, she took two steps inside. Immediately, the delicious aroma of roast beef and freshly baked bread greeted her. Her mouth watered.

"*Señorita Andrea!*" A small, round-faced Mexican woman turned from her place by the cast-iron cookstove and regarded Andi with a look of disapproval. She shook her head and tossed a gray-streaked black braid behind her shoulder. "*Tu mamá está muy preocupada.*"

Andi didn't doubt Mother was worried. Her youngest daughter had disappeared without a word and been gone all day.

Luisa placed her hands on her hips. "Where have you been?" She rattled off in Spanish so fast that Andi could hardly keep up with her, even though she spoke the language fluently. "Your mama held supper for you, but you didn't come home. And *Señor* Chad came in awfully upset about you this afternoon."

Andi grimaced and headed for the sink, trying hard to ignore Luisa's scolding. Hearing that her mother had held supper sent a message of hope to her gnawing stomach. If she hurried, she might make most of the meal. She gave two quick jerks to the kitchen pump and thrust her hands under the water. A few seconds later she was drying them off on a nearby towel.

Luisa's dark eyes widened. She threw up her hands in dismay. "*¡Ay, no, señorita!* That is not good enough for tonight. You must clean up and change your clothes before you—"

"I'll miss what's left of supper if I do that." Andi tossed the towel onto the counter and headed for the dining room. "And I'm starved."

"*Señorita*, wait!" Luisa called after her. "There's company . . ." Her voice trailed off.

Andi burst through the door and into the dining room at a dead run. She blurted out her apologies before looking around. "I heard you held supper for me, Mother. I'm sorry I'm late. I lost track of the time."

She caught sight of her oldest brother and stopped short. "Justin! When did you get back?" With a delighted grin, she rushed over and threw her arms around his neck. "I'm so glad you're home. I've got *so* much to tell you. You won't believe what happened today. Do you know what Chad said to me?" She made a face. "I suppose he had good reason, but he didn't need to shout like a—"

"Andrea."

Andi spun around at the sound of her mother's quiet voice. Her smile faded when she saw a stranger sitting between Chad and Mitch. In her hurry to greet Justin, she hadn't noticed their dinner guest.

The stranger was a distinguished-looking man with brown eyes and neatly combed silver hair. His clothes and manner shouted the words *important visitor* as clearly as if he were holding up a sign.

For the first time, Andi looked closely at the rest of her family. Her mother and sister were dressed in their Sunday best. Her brothers wore suits.

Andi's heart sank to her toes.

"Hello there." The stranger broke the awkward silence. His eyes twinkled merrily at her.

Andi's face grew hot. She backed away from Justin and glanced down at herself in horror. Her overalls were grass-stained and streaked with dried mud. Her shirttail hung out, wrinkled and dirty, and the sleeves were rolled up past her elbows. Her hair, which had started the day as two braids, now hung in long, wild tangles. Small pieces of grass and flower petals speckled the dark, wavy mass, bearing silent evidence of an afternoon spent in the meadow.

Justin recovered first. He stood up, put his arm around Andi's shoulder, and gave her an affectionate hug. "Jim, I would like you to meet my youngest sister, Andrea." He turned to Andi. "Honey, this is Senator James Farley, visiting from Washington. He's out West for a few weeks, making a tour of the state he's supposed to be representing." He grinned.

"I'm delighted to make your acquaintance, Miss Carter." The senator stood and gave Andi a polite nod.

"Pleased to meet you," Andi whispered, not pleased at all. She made the tiniest fraction of a curtsy, which wasn't easy to do while wearing overalls. *A senator from the nation's capital.* She gulped. *Oh, what must he be thinking?*

Senator Farley smiled and sat down. He indicated the empty seat next to Melinda. "Please join us, Miss Carter. I would certainly enjoy hearing how you spent your afternoon."

Andi turned to her mother in dismay.

"You should first make yourself presentable, don't you think?"

"Yes, Mother," Andi quickly agreed. She gathered what was left of her shattered dignity and turned to Senator Farley. "If you'll excuse me, please?"

The senator nodded, and Andi hurried from the room. Once out of sight, she paused to hear her mother's apology and the senator's deep chuckle. "Please don't apologize, Mrs. Carter." He laughed again. "It brightened my day."

Andi waited to hear no more. She raced through the foyer and took the stairs two at a time. Then she slammed the door to her room and collapsed onto her bed in misery. *I'm never going back down there. Never!* She rolled over and stared at the ceiling. Her empty stomach rumbled a protest to her declaration.

The knock on her door a minute later startled Andi, who had done nothing to make herself presentable. She sprang up, stripped off her overalls, and slipped a petticoat over her head. As she reached for a suitable dress, a second knock—more insistent this time—sounded. The door opened.

"Andrea?" Her mother walked in and closed the door behind her.

Andi sat down on her bed and let the dress fall from her hand. "Oh, Mother! How could Justin do this to me? He didn't tell us he was coming home today. And he brought a *senator*. How could he?"

Elizabeth joined her daughter on the bed. "Justin sent a telegram.

It arrived just before noon. I looked for you in the barn so I could share the good news, but you weren't there. Nobody knew where you were."

That struck Andi to the heart. "I'm sorry. It's been a miserable day."

"So I've heard. Chad told me about it this afternoon. I'm shocked. But running off instead of finishing your chores didn't solve a thing, did it?"

Andi frowned. "It made me feel better."

"You're not supposed to feel better. You're supposed to learn from it, be thankful Chad loves you enough to watch out for you, and do your chores without getting into trouble."

Andi shook her head. "But he was so angry with me. I didn't know what to say. He threatened to *spank* me." She scowled at the memory.

"I know all about it," Elizabeth said.

Andi hung her head. "I'm sorry, Mother. I can't do anything right these days."

"It certainly appears that way." She turned her head, taking in her daughter's room.

Andi followed her mother's gaze and bit her lip. Her room was exactly as she had left it—the bed unmade, yesterday's school clothes hanging carelessly over a chair, and her nightgown lying in a heap on the floor. Books and papers lay atop her chest of drawers, which stood open. A dusty saddle blanket, discarded in a corner, completed the unappealing scene.

"I hardly know what to do with you, Andrea," her mother continued. "Forgetting your chores is one thing, but disregarding Chad's instructions about the stallion is inexcusable. He's only trying to protect you."

Andi clenched her fists. "He doesn't have to be so bossy about it."

Her mother shook her head and gave Andi a firm look. "You are in the wrong on all accounts, and I want to see some improvement. *Quickly.* Do you understand?"

Andi nodded and looked at the floor.

"All right, then. Finish dressing and come down to supper." She sighed. "You can straighten your room later."

Andi's head snapped up. "I can't go down. Not with the senator there. He was laughing at me, like I was nothing but a dirty, silly tomboy."

Andi's mother rose from the bed. "If you don't want people to think you're a tomboy, don't come to the table looking like one." She made her way to the door. "I expect you to be ready to eat in five minutes."

"I'm not hungry."

"All right. You needn't eat. But you *will* join the rest of the family."

"Mother, *please*."

Elizabeth turned to regard her daughter one last time. "As soon as you've made yourself presentable in a manner which honors our guest, you will come downstairs and join us for the remainder of the evening meal." The look on her mother's face kept Andi from interrupting. "In this family, no one is allowed to be a coward because of a little embarrassment."

She opened the door and turned for a final word. "Don't disappoint me in this, Andrea."

The door closed.

Andi was left with no choice but to do as her mother asked.

Chapter Four

EAVESDROPPER

Andi joined her family in the dining room a few minutes later, dressed in her best and quiet to a fault. She found her seat next to Melinda, sat down, and began dishing up a helping of meat and potatoes.

She didn't dare look at the senator. Amusement had danced in his eyes during her introduction earlier. He was surely thinking all sorts of unflattering things about her and the poor reflection she must be on her family.

"I'm delighted you could join us, Miss Carter," Senator Farley remarked with a twinkle in his eyes. "I can't help but admire the remarkable transformation you made so quickly. My daughter Sophia takes an endless amount of time to simply ready herself for school, and she has her own maid." He chuckled.

Andi reddened at his words. Transformation? Oh, yes. Her transformation from wild and reckless tomboy into a young lady with perfect manners.

She acknowledged the senator's remark with a polite nod but said nothing. She went back to her meal without glancing up.

The conversation flowed around Andi in a soft murmur. She was grateful for that and hoped she could finish quickly and be allowed to escape back to her room or—better yet—Taffy's stall.

Andi listened idly when Melinda asked the senator about the

32

latest styles in the nation's capital and heard him respond with genuine interest. A few minutes later Andi heard polite laughter over some ranch-related story Mitch told. She was almost ready to admit that supper perhaps wasn't a disaster, after all.

She pricked up her ears at Justin's next remark. "Say, Chad. Speaking of what's new on the ranch since I've been away, I see you finally got hold of that stallion you've been itching to buy. Did it cost you as much as you figured?"

Chad laughed. "More, actually. But he's worth it."

"How is he working out? I know the senator would enjoy a demonstration of what you've accomplished." He turned to Senator Farley. "What Chad can't do with a horse can't be done, Jim."

"I would certainly be interested in an exhibition," the senator agreed. "I saw the horse briefly when we rode up." He whistled. "Gorgeous animal."

"He has a few rough edges," came Chad's hesitant reply. "I'm afraid he won't be up to any kind of display within the next few days. He's still jittery."

Andi groaned inwardly. Justin had chosen the worst possible subject for table talk. She caught Chad's troubled look. *Please change the subject*, she pleaded with her eyes.

Justin plunged on. "Is that where the new corral fence came from? His rough edges?" He waved his hand in the direction of the yard. "I saw the new railing on the section closest to the barn."

Of course you did, Andi thought. Her oldest brother never missed anything. That's what made him an excellent attorney.

"He didn't break out, did he?" Now Justin sounded concerned. "That would be too bad if he did."

"No." Chad glanced at Andi then looked away. "He didn't break out. There was an unexpected concern this morning, but I got it under control."

Andi held her breath. If Chad didn't watch himself, the reason for the stallion's bad behavior today would come out, shaming Andi even more.

No matter how often they argued, Andi knew Chad loved her. He would not be interested in letting her foolish actions from this morning be aired more publicly than they already had been. The ranch hands were acquainted with Andi's shortcomings. The senator was not.

"Well," Justin continued, helping himself to seconds, "so long as the stallion doesn't get out. No telling what could happen if—"

"I said I have it under control."

Chad's clipped reply silenced Justin. He frowned, clearly taken aback at his brother's tone. Not even the senator could miss the tension in the air. It felt thick enough to cut with a knife.

"Please pass the biscuits, Andi," Mitch said cheerfully.

Andi relaxed. Leave it to Mitch to smooth things over. She handed the plate to Melinda, who passed it along.

Senator Farley smiled across the table. "And you, Andrea? What do you think of your brother's new stallion?"

Not the stallion again! Why couldn't Senator Farley and her brothers go back to talking about politics or other dull affairs back East? "He's all right," she answered with a disinterested shrug.

The senator chuckled. "Just *all right*, Miss Carter? He's more than that, I think. Living on such a grand ranch, you must certainly like horses. Or am I mistaken?"

Andi nodded. "Yes, sir, I do." She ducked her head, but not before she caught Justin's piercing look. *What's going on?*

She ignored him. "May I please be excused, Mother?"

Elizabeth nodded.

Andi escaped from the dining room as fast as her legs could carry her. She closed her bedroom door, leaned against it, and slid weakly to the floor. "I'm glad *that's* over." At least her stomach was full. It was the only good thing she could say about the awkward meal.

Senator Farley had looked disappointed when Andi asked to be excused, but not another minute would she sit and wait for the senator to ask more horse-related questions. Sooner or later, the stallion would gallop back into the conversation.

"Why is that fancy senator so interested in talking to *me*?" she muttered.

Andi spent the remainder of the evening in her room, out of sight of Senator Farley and his laughing eyes. With any luck, she could avoid him tomorrow by eating an early breakfast. She wouldn't have to sit near him in church. Afterward, maybe he'd be gone.

"But that means Justin will go back to Sacramento too," she said mournfully. Andi didn't want that to happen—at least not until she had talked with him. If she waited long enough, Justin would come up to say good night. Whenever he was home, he made a point of spending time with his youngest sister. She had come to expect it.

Andi looked forward to telling her brother all about her miserable day. He would listen patiently, sympathize with her, and then give her the same advice Mother had given her. Somehow, it always sounded better coming from Justin.

The sound of the grandfather clock downstairs striking the hour caused Andi to look up from the book she was reading. She glanced at her own small clock. Eleven o'clock. "What can be keeping Justin?" she wondered, slipping from her bed.

Andi cracked open the bedroom door and listened for the murmur of conversation coming from below. She wasn't the least bit tired, having slept away the afternoon. She crept to the top of the stairs to hear what was so terribly important that Justin couldn't pull himself away for a few minutes to say good night.

"We've got to think of something, and soon." As usual, Chad wasn't bothering to keep his voice down.

"Chad," Mother said. "Your voice, please. I doubt Senator Farley appreciates your bellowing when he's trying to sleep."

"All right." Chad lowered his voice a fraction. "Something's got to be done about Andi."

His words sent Andi scurrying behind the banister. She wrapped her shaking fingers around the railings and held her breath.

"Can't this wait until morning?" Justin asked.

"No. You're home, and I want your advice before you take off for Sacramento again," Chad said. "I've got enough on my mind this time of year without having to check up on Andi. Most days I'm either redoing her chores or pulling her out of trouble."

There was a slight pause, and Chad plowed on. "Remember what happened last week, Mitch? Sid McCoy dragged Andi home after he nearly ran her over with a group of geldings he was bringing in. The horses scattered, and it cost him and his men half a day's work to round them up again."

Andi's cheeks grew warm. That had been a horrible day. She hadn't meant to startle the small herd, but—

"Sid gave me an earful about it. When my foreman starts grumbling, I've got to listen."

Justin sighed. "It can't be as bad as you're making out. You're always extra irritated this time of year. Why don't you let her help? She's pretty good with a lasso."

"Let her help?" Chad's voice rose. "Easy for you to say, lawyer-man. You haven't been around lately. She hasn't earned anything close to the right to help this spring. The stallion was the last straw. She could have been killed."

"It was pretty scary," Mitch admitted. "I aged ten years watching Chad creep up on her. I don't want to see something like that again."

"Mother?" Justin ventured.

"I'd be grateful for some suggestions." Mother sounded sad, frustrated, and helpless, all rolled into one. "Andrea usually listens to you, Justin. I don't know what's come over her lately. She doesn't stop to think about consequences—just plunges headlong into things."

Tears pricked Andi's eyes. *I don't do it on purpose!*

"I'll talk to her," Justin said. "But it sounds exactly like you at that age, Chad." He chuckled. "I remember Father getting after you all the time. The good news? You grew out of it, and Andi will too. Be patient. She just needs a little time to grow up."

"And in the meantime?" Chad asked. "How do I keep her safe? Any suggestions for getting her head out of the clouds and back to where it belongs?"

Silence.

"That's what I thought." Chad let out a long breath. "It's going to take more than talking and waiting, big brother. I've thought about it, and I think Andi should spend some time in the city with Aunt Rebecca."

Andi covered her mouth to keep her frightened gasp inside. Her free hand gripped the railing until her knuckles turned white. How could Chad suggest such a thing? Visit Aunt Rebecca? *No!*

"You can't be serious." Justin sounded astonished.

"I'm perfectly serious," Chad replied. "I don't think it would hurt Andi one bit to cool her heels in San Francisco for a couple of months. Aunt Rebecca lives in that enormous house all alone, except for half a dozen servants. She's written countless times, inviting the girls for a visit. There's plenty to do and see there. If I'm not mistaken, there's a girls' school not too far away. Andi could finish up the spring term and be kept out of trouble."

"I'd be happy to go along," Melinda offered. "I haven't been to the city in ages. That way Andi wouldn't have to go alone."

Andi blinked back tears of fury and helplessness. Her family was planning her entire future without even asking her. *I despise the city!*

"I don't think it's a good idea," Justin said. "There must be another solution, preferably one closer to home." He paused. "Mother, surely you're not in agreement with this?"

Andi strained to hear her mother's soft-spoken reply. If Mother agreed with the ranch boss, then off to San Francisco Andi would go—whether she wanted to or not.

"Eavesdroppers sometimes hear things they shouldn't."

A voice barely above a whisper jerked Andi around. Senator Farley stood above her, gazing thoughtfully over the banister into the foyer below. She knew he couldn't see into the large sitting room, but the voices coming from it were crystal clear.

"I . . . I . . ." Andi choked on her words. A United States senator had caught her in the disgraceful act of eavesdropping on her family. She half expected the man to call out over the railing and reveal her presence or to reprimand her himself.

The senator did neither. Instead, he stood quietly and regarded her with a look of compassion. "Believe me, Miss Carter. Everything will look better in the morning."

Andi could think of nothing to say. Her tongue felt glued to the roof of her mouth. Tossing all courtesy aside, she jumped up and fled to her room, shutting the door quietly behind her. Then she threw herself across her bed and dissolved into inconsolable tears.

When her tears no longer came, Andi wiped her eyes and sat up. She plucked at her coverlet, thinking hard. It was obvious she was a lot of trouble to everyone on the ranch. Until tonight, she hadn't realized just how *much* trouble.

Enough trouble to be sent away to the city. Andi groaned. The words "Aunt Rebecca" and "girls' school" plunged her into gut-wrenching fear. "I'll die if I'm cooped up in San Francisco with Aunt Rebecca. She's always trying to turn me into a prissy young lady." Andi shuddered. "And I couldn't bear to be sent off to some girls' school."

She clenched her fists and brought them down against the bed. "How can Chad even consider it?" She shook her head. "He must still be awfully sore about that stallion. He's sure to convince Mother it would be good for me to go to Aunt Rebecca's."

The thought of being sent to San Francisco brought fresh tears trickling down Andi's cheeks. She loved the ranch as much as anyone in her family. Nothing could take the place of feeling the sun and wind on her face or smelling the freshly cut hay. The friendly sounds of the cowboys working with the cattle or the plaintive cry of a lost calf were the sounds of home to her.

Andi turned cold inside at the thought of staying with her spinster aunt for more than a few days. One visit to San Francisco when she was nine years old had been enough to convince her she hated it—all those tall buildings stacked next to each other, closing her in so she could scarcely breathe.

No, she determined fiercely, *not if I can help it.*

Chapter Five

INTO THE NIGHT

A ndi lay awake pondering for several hours. Part of her hoped Mother or Justin would come upstairs and assure her that their earlier conversation had been nothing more than a storm of words. Chad blustered, Mother listened patiently, but it was Justin who always came through with a sensible answer.

Another part of Andi's mind whispered the truth, however. She had crossed the line today with her disobedience. She'd not only endangered her own life, but she had also put the ranch hands at risk when they tried to calm the stallion.

No, Chad would not be forgetting this incident any time soon. Justin would be off tomorrow or the next day. He wouldn't be any help, not from faraway Sacramento. And Mother? Andi sighed. Mother let Chad make all the ranch decisions. If Andi had been a ranch hand, Chad would have fired her on the spot.

I reckon I have to figure this out on my own, Andi decided. *But I know one thing. I can't go to San Francisco.*

A few hours before dawn, Andi saddled Taffy, tied up her bedroll, and slipped some supplies into her saddlebags. No one was up, not even the hired hands. The ranch lay in quiet tranquility. Only the occasional rustling of the treetops broke the stillness.

Andi glanced at her home one more time. Then she turned and

led her horse silently out of the yard, through the gate, and onto the road that led west toward town.

She adjusted her wide-brimmed, black felt hat and pulled it down securely over her forehead. It felt awkward and uncomfortable with her hair stuffed tightly inside, but she knew a strong young boy had a much better chance of finding and keeping a job than a girl. Boots, overalls, and a warm jacket completed the illusion.

Andi rubbed her watery eyes. She'd return home in a couple of weeks, once all the fuss had settled down. Chad just needed time to cool off—probably more time than usual. A week or ten days would be long enough for her family to get over the idea of sending her to Aunt Rebecca.

"I'm not going far," she told Taffy. The next town couldn't be more than a day's ride from the ranch. Perhaps her family would miss her and come after her. Maybe they'd forget about the trouble she'd stirred up. She could start over.

A little voice in her head warned her she would be sorry if she left, but she pushed the thought into a corner of her mind. A louder voice took over. She couldn't get into trouble if she wasn't around. Chad couldn't boss her and tell her what to do all the time. She would be free.

Andi mounted her palomino and gripped the reins. "Come on, Taffy. Let's get out of here."

She didn't look back.

Ⓒ

The two travelers had no trouble seeing their way through the mild spring night. The full moon bathed the road in silver light. Andi was familiar enough with this particular stretch of road to know there were no surprises awaiting her. She traveled it several times a week to school.

It was a pleasant road, bordered on both sides by acres and acres of young orchards. Only a few short weeks ago the trees were bursting with blossoms. Now all that remained was a carpet of pink and white. The discarded petals glistened in the moonlight like a layer of freshly fallen snow.

The road to town was a long one. Nearly an hour passed before Andi could make out the shadows of the outlying buildings that marked the edge of Fresno. She grew alert when she entered the town. It wouldn't do to be caught, especially by the sheriff. He would drag her home in disgrace and she'd never hear the end of it. Being caught by one of his deputies would be just as bad, so she kept a sharp lookout for any movement in the streets.

She soon discovered she had worried for nothing. The town slumbered in the quiet hours before dawn. The saloons were closed, and the shopkeepers wouldn't open at all on Sunday morning. If the sheriff and his deputies were making their rounds, they were making them someplace else.

Andi heard and saw nothing.

Once through town, she turned south and gave Taffy her head. She'd heard that numerous little towns dotted this part of the valley. Any one of them might hold an opportunity to make some money and find a place to stay. Unfortunately, Andi had never been south of Fresno before. She had no idea how far the next town actually was.

Andi had left Fresno several miles to the north when night began to give way to a pale, cloudless dawn. She yawned and tried to stretch. She pulled her feet from the stirrups and brought one leg up around the pommel of her saddle—anything to stay awake and get comfortable. Weariness lay over Andi like a heavy blanket. The steady *clip-clop* of Taffy's hooves added to her drowsiness.

How far is it to the next town? Andi didn't favor being seen by the stagecoach driver, who was bound to be along a few hours after the sun rose. Although it was doubtful he'd recognize her, he'd surely remember a golden palomino and a boy if questioned by the sheriff later on.

Taffy's sudden alertness pulled Andi from her sleepy thoughts. She sat up and slipped her feet back into the stirrups. "What is it, girl?" she whispered.

"Howdy," a loud, invisible voice hailed her.

Andi pulled back on the reins. All sleepiness vanished. "Who's there?" The moon had set, and she strained to see through the dim light of the approaching dawn. A stab of uncertainty set her heart racing.

The owner of the voice stepped into sight. He was a man of medium height and build, leading a sorry-looking horse that appeared to be lame.

"Howdy, young fella. I sure am glad to see you." The man grinned and shoved his hat back, allowing Andi a better look at him. Friendly blue eyes in a clean-shaven face stared up at her. "This has got to be the longest night of my life."

"H-howdy." Andi cautiously returned the stranger's greeting, lowering her voice to sound like a boy.

The man stepped closer. "Where're you headed?"

Andi didn't answer. She tightened the reins and backed Taffy up. Her heart pounded against the inside of her chest.

"Wait, boy." The man held up both hands and spread them apart. "Don't run off. I'm really stuck. My horse found a hole and went lame on me. I've been walking for hours. Do you know how far it is to the next town?"

Andi began to relax at the man's open, easygoing manner. Her heart slowed down, and she breathed easier. "It's a couple of hours' riding time back that way to Fresno." She pointed behind her shoulder. "But it's a lot longer if you're walking. You're better off finding a place to rest alongside the road. The stage should be by in an hour or two. The driver might pick you up."

The stranger shook his head. "I dunno. I'd much rather get hold of another horse." He grew quiet and narrowed his eyes. His gaze swept over Andi's horse and tack.

She swallowed. Taffy was a fine horse—one of her family's best. Andi shifted uneasily in her saddle and gripped the reins with a shaky hand.

The man reached out and patted Taffy on the chest. He gave a low whistle. "Where did you get this horse, boy? Sure is a beauty."

"She's mine." Andi urged Taffy back a few more steps. The mare whinnied. "Easy, girl," Andi soothed her.

The stranger laughed and backed off. He folded his arms and grinned up at Andi. "You wanna sell me the horse? I'll even throw this old nag in for free." He waved toward the lame animal.

"No."

"Aw, come on, kid. I'm sure you didn't pay for her. Any fool can see that's a rich man's horse and tack." He drew closer, and his voice dropped to a whisper. "Why else would a boy your size be riding around in the middle of the night? Did you steal the mare from your boss?" He gave a low chuckle. "You sure picked a fine animal. I'll give you fifty dollars, no questions asked. That's a lot of money for a boy."

Andi stared at the man, speechless with shock. When she found her voice, it shook with alarm. "What do you mean?" She jerked Taffy around. It was long past time to get away from this drifter. "I'm not selling you my horse." She leaned forward and prepared to gallop away.

The man reached out with amazing speed and grabbed the reins. Taffy reared up in fear, but he yanked her down. His fist curled around the bridle. "I'm taking this horse, boy"—he was no longer smiling—"with or without your say-so."

Cold fear stabbed Andi like a knife. Her morning encounter with Chad's stallion hadn't frightened her anywhere near as much as this stranger scared her now.

In the space of a few seconds, Andi came to understand her

brother's point of view regarding so many things that to her own mind had seemed mean and bossy. Mother was right. Chad was only trying to protect her from dangerous situations—like with the stallion—and from dangerous people—like this one.

I'm going home, she decided in a heartbeat. She wanted to fly into Chad's arms and promise she'd never disobey him as ranch boss ever again. She was even willing to stay with Aunt Rebecca for a few weeks. Anything to be away from this—

"Get off the horse," the drifter growled. "I won't ask you again."

The terror of losing Taffy propelled Andi into action. "Let go of my horse!" She yanked on the reins and dug her heels into Taffy's flank.

The mare leaped forward, but the stranger gripped the bridle and hung on. "Fool kid," he muttered.

With his free hand, the man reached out and wrenched Andi from the saddle. He flung her into the rocks and brush that lined the side of the road.

Andi landed with a crash and everything faded to black.

Chapter Six

NEW FRIENDS

A ndi woke with a groan and tried to sit up. Her head exploded into a thousand pinpricks. A pair of gentle but firm hands prevented her from rising, and a voice spoke in soothing tones.

"Acuéstate, chiquita." The Spanish words sounded strange, yet familiar, and Andi lay down in obedience to the command. Her head immediately felt better.

Slowly, Andi opened her eyes, being careful not to move. Gazing down at her was the friendly, open face of a Mexican woman. Her dark eyes showed her relief at finding Andi awake. *"Buenos días."*

"Buenos días, señora," Andi replied. *"¿Dónde estoy?"*

Astonishment filled the woman's face. "You speak Spanish."

"Sí," came Andi's anxious reply. *Where am I? What happened?*

"That is good," the woman said with a smile, "because we speak no English."

"Please, where am I?" Andi repeated in Spanish.

"You are with the Garduño family. I am Nila. It has been many hours since my husband found you on the road. You were hurt and unconscious. He brought you here to our camp. I cleaned and bandaged a deep cut on your head. What happened?"

Andi frowned and tried to piece together the past few hours. Darkness. A man's rough voice. Fear. Taffy. She caught her breath. *Where's Taffy?* "My horse! I remember riding Taffy, but not much else." She looked around the camp. "Did you bring my horse here too?"

"*Lo siento.*" Nila shook her head in apology. "We found only you. No horse."

"Oh, no." Guilt washed over Andi. If Taffy was lost or stolen because of her foolish running off, she would never forgive herself. "I don't remember anything else."

"Not to worry, little one. It is likely everything will return in a day or two." Nila patted her gently on the arm. "If you tell us your name, we can return you to your family. They must be worried about you."

"It's Andrea."

"Andrea? That's all? Just Andrea?"

"Please, *señora*, I don't want you to return me to my family. Not yet. Not until I find my horse."

"But your *mamá*, your *papá!*"

"No. Thank you, *señora*, for what you've done already. If you'll take me back to the place you found me, I can start searching for Taffy. Please."

"But, child, you have nothing. No horse, no money, no decent clothes." She waved a scoffing hand toward the overalls hanging over the back of the wagon. "Those are the clothes of a boy, not of a young lady."

"I know," Andi agreed. "I thought it would be safer to travel as a boy."

The woman chuckled and shook her head. "Not many would mistake you for a boy, no matter what you're wearing." She reached out and grasped a handful of Andi's tangled mass of dark waves. "Even if you were to cut your hair, it would not help, for you do not look or speak like a boy. Your speech is gracious and educated—like one would expect from a young lady of good family."

Andi groaned. She had counted on her disguise.

"Never mind, *chiquita*," Nila said. "You may stay here for the present, at least until you are fully recovered. It is unthinkable that we would allow you to wander off with no protection."

She gave Nila a grateful smile. *"Gracias."*

"I will tell the others you have finally awakened. Would you like to meet my family? The children are very curious."

Andi nodded and closed her eyes, suddenly exhausted.

Nila sighed. "I think perhaps my family will meet you later. You must rest first and recover." She tucked a worn quilt around Andi and smiled. "Have no fear, little one. The Garduño family will care for you and see you safely returned to your family. That is a promise."

The sounds of laughter and play awakened Andi. She opened her eyes and found herself in the back of a small wagon, sprawled out on a bed of mounded quilts and blankets. Overhead a grove of cottonwood trees waved in the afternoon breeze, their new leaves green against the sky. In the distance she heard friendly chatter and the occasional braying of a donkey. They were pleasant sounds.

Andi propped herself up on one elbow and looked over the side. She saw a camp. Whether it was permanent or temporary, she couldn't tell. The fire was being tended by the Mexican woman, Nila, who was frying tortillas with a deft hand. Andi's mouth watered and her stomach growled.

"Buenas tardes," a strange voice uttered.

Andi whirled. A young girl not much older than herself was staring at her. "Good afternoon," Andi replied in Spanish. "Who are you?"

"I'm Rosa," the girl answered with a smile. "And you're Andrea."

"That's right."

"How do you feel?"

"Much better. My head hurts only a little." She grinned. "What is he doing with that burro?" She pointed to a small gray donkey and a boy struggling with it.

"My brother is trying to hold him still long enough to get on,"

Rosa replied. "Joselito dreams of becoming *un gran vaquero* someday." She giggled. "He uses our burro to practice riding. Watch."

Andi held her breath as the boy threw himself onto the donkey's back. The little beast looked surprised for a second before kicking up its heels. Joselito flew between the burro's ears and landed facedown in the dirt.

Andi hid a smile behind her hand. The Mexican boy appeared far from becoming the grand cowboy of his dreams.

The donkey brayed and took off running.

"He's getting away," Andi exclaimed.

"Don't worry. He never goes far. A little corn always brings him back."

"I see you are much better, *chiquita*." Nila's voice broke into the girls' conversation. She reached out and gently drew the white cloth from around Andi's head. She examined the gash, nodded in satisfaction, and replaced the cloth. "Yes. Much better. How does your head feel this afternoon?"

"I have a headache, but it's nothing like earlier today. Thank you again."

Nila indicated the campfire. "Are you hungry? We have fresh tortillas and beans."

"I'm starved." Although her head still ached from her accident, it didn't make Andi want to stay in bed, and she wasn't dizzy. She glanced around for her overalls, but they had mysteriously vanished. "Where are my overalls?"

Nila dismissed Andi's question with a wave of her hand. "Your things are not suitable for a young lady. Joselito will get much better use from them than you."

Andi wrapped the quilt more tightly around her shoulders. "Then what am I to wear?" She could not insult this kind woman by demanding her clothes be returned, but her thoughts whirled. *Does she expect me to keep this blanket wrapped around my undergarments all day?*

Nila smiled and held up a worn but still colorful skirt and a plain white blouse. "You may wear these for now."

Andi nodded her thanks and slipped into the strange clothes.

Nila offered Andi a helping hand. "Now, come."

Andi carefully made her way over the back of the wagon and onto the ground. As her bare feet touched the warm dust, she winced. Every muscle in her body ached. She steadied herself against the wagon.

"Are you all right?" Rosa asked.

"I'm fine," Andi insisted, even though she felt suddenly fatigued. She couldn't lie around in bed. She had to find Taffy.

Nila led Andi to the fire and helped settle her on a fallen log. She heaped a generous portion of beans and tortillas onto a tin plate and handed it to Andi, along with a steaming cup of coffee. Her face showed her pleasure when Andi devoured the offering.

"Now that your stomach is content," another voice began, "perhaps you would be kind enough to tell us your story—who you are and where you are from."

Andi swallowed the last of her coffee and turned to look at the owner of the voice. He was a tall, middle-aged man with a mustache, wearing the loose cotton pants and shirt typical of Mexican peasants. He had a serious, honest face, and the look of one who had seen his share of hardships. He stood before Andi, waiting patiently for her reply as he chewed on a tortilla and sipped his coffee.

"Now, José," Nila warned, rising from her seat. "I told you the child must not be pestered about such things. She is recovering from a head injury."

"I only wish to know where she lives, so we can return her to her family," José replied pleasantly.

"But—"

José lowered his cup of coffee. "Wife, I do not like mysteries." He pointed to Andi. "And this young girl has been a mystery ever since I found her. She worries me. We are newly come to the United

States and do not understand the customs or the people. We do not know who this girl is or where she's from. Such things could be dangerous." He turned to Andi, and his voice softened. "I mean no disrespect to you, *señorita*, but I would be grateful for some answers."

"Sí, señor," Andi agreed. "But please don't make me tell you where I'm from. I must first find my horse—my best friend."

"I see. So, you will not tell us your name?"

"It's Andrea. I told the *señora* already."

"How did you come to be on the road?"

Rest and good food had restored Andi's memory, just like Nila had hinted. "I met a drifter on the road last night. He wanted to buy my horse. I"—Andi swallowed—"I refused. I think he took her anyway. It all happened so fast. I tried to get away, but . . ."

Andi's voice trailed away as she relived the horrible memory of losing Taffy. She looked up at José. "I have to find my horse before I go home. I can't go back without her."

"You are so sure of this?"

"Sí," Andi answered. Never in a thousand years would she return and face Chad without Taffy.

José swallowed the rest of his coffee and set down his tin cup. When he spoke again, his voice was gentle but firm. "What were you doing on the road in the middle of the night? Why were you not at home where you and your horse belong?"

It was the question Andi had been dreading, and the one for which she had no good answer. "I left." She bowed her head in shame.

"You left home?" José probed patiently. "Why? Were you mistreated?"

Andi shook her head. "No." Her eyes welled up with tears. How foolish she'd been! "I was angry. I didn't slow down long enough to think about what I was doing. I just ran."

"I see," José murmured in a voice that sounded as if he understood all too well.

Andi rubbed her eyes and tried to swallow the lump forming in her throat. "Now I've lost my horse," she cried, unable to hold the tears back any longer.

"José!" Nila cried out, rushing to her. "See what you have done." She pulled Andi into a tender embrace and rocked her. The two Garduño children watched with wide eyes, their food untouched.

José sighed. "Look at me, child."

Andi looked up and sniffed back her tears.

"I do not mean to be harsh," José said, "but it is a dangerous thing for a young girl to be wandering alone in the open country. You belong under the protection of your family, where you are safe." He smiled. "You are fortunate, however, to have fallen in with us. Tomorrow morning we will take you back to your family. They will understand. A good family always does. You will be scolded, then forgiven, and all will be as before."

"It *won't* be as before!" Andi jumped up. She winced when her head protested her sudden movement. "I can't go back. Not without my horse. I could never hurt my brother like that. He gave me Taffy when I was six years old. It would kill him to see what I've done. I allowed my best friend to be stolen. All because I was feeling sorry for myself."

She faced José and took a deep breath. The Garduño family had been kind, but Andi could not—*would* not—go home without Taffy at her side. "I'm sorry, but I won't tell you where I live. If you return my own clothes, I'll be on my way."

"No, child." José shook his head. "We cannot allow you to go off on your own. I see you are a headstrong girl and this horse means much to you—too much for you to see clearly." He let out a weary breath, as if he would soon regret his next words. "If you like, you may stay with us for the time being. Perhaps we will come across your horse. After all, it has been less than a day."

"*¡Gracias, señor! ¡Gracias!* You won't be sorry. I'll work hard to pay for my food. Anything you ask. And I promise when I find my horse, I'll gallop home as fast as I can and ask to be forgiven, like the prodigal son in the Bible." She grinned. "Except I'm a *daughter*."

José nodded. "Good. Now, I think there may be a way you can help us."

"How?" Andi asked, eager to please.

"You are an American and speak English, yes?"

Andi frowned at the unexpected question. "Yes."

José broke into a wide smile. "That is good. We are at a disadvantage here in California. Because we cannot speak the language, many *gringos* cheat us when we try to buy supplies. They pay us far too little for our work, or sometimes not at all."

His look turned serious. "Would you be willing to teach us English and speak for us to the *gringos* in exchange for food and clothing—and, of course, for our aid in the search for your horse?"

Andi nodded. *"Sí, señor. ¡Con mucho gusto!"*

Chapter Seven

SECOND THOUGHTS

Andi gazed across the field of beans and groaned. It looked identical to the other fields that she and the Garduño family had worked the past week.

"I got only a few days' work for ya, that's all," a loud, hurried voice was saying. The voice belonged to a heavyset, overalls-clad farmer. He chewed a generous wad of tobacco, swirling it round and round in his cheek. With practiced aim, he spat a brown stream at José's feet. He grinned and continued.

"Most o' this field's been picked already by me an' my young'uns. I'd be finishin' up if it weren't for this bad back o' mine and the fact that the young'uns come down with the ague. Got the chills real bad." He spat again, this time at Nila's feet. "Can't pay ya much. The missus'll give your woman some grub for your family. What d'ya say?"

José glanced down at Andi with a questioning look. In rapid Spanish, she told him all the farmer had said. José looked out across the field, took a deep breath, and nodded. *"Bueno. ¿Adónde vamos?"*

Andi turned to the farmer. "All right. Where do we go?"

The man pulled up his work-worn overalls, adjusted his slouch hat, and shot another stream of tobacco juice. He waved a dirt-encrusted hand toward a small stand of cottonwoods about fifty yards away. "See them trees 'cross the field?"

Andi nodded.

"That's the creek. Start there an' work your way back t' the barn. Got some wood that needs choppin' too, and a couple stalls t' be mucked out." He grinned down at Andi and Rosa. "Can ya handle a pitchfork?"

Andi bit her lip and nodded.

"And you, boy." The farmer waved toward Joselito. "You can fill the wood box for the missus, then get out in the fields with your folks."

"He wants you to chop wood," Andi told the boy in Spanish. "Afterward, you can join your parents."

Joselito nodded and headed for the woodpile.

The farmer squinted into the early morning sunshine. "Gonna be a hot one t' day." He turned to the Mexican family. "Come see me at sundown. The missus'll get ya your grub." He frowned. "Well, what're ya waitin' fer? Get t' work."

This time, José needed no translation. He snatched up a couple of empty bushel baskets and headed for the field. Nila followed with a basket in each hand.

"Come with me," the farmer commanded Andi and Rosa. "I gotta hitch up the team so your folks kin load the baskets. I'll show ya the stalls that need muckin' out."

Andi and Rosa followed the dirty farmer into a barn that looked ready to collapse. It was musty inside, and dark except for the strips of sunlight shining through wide cracks between the weathered planks. Barely four feet above their heads, a sagging loft threatened to tumble down on them. Small pieces of last summer's hay drifted through cracks and into their hair.

With a grunt, the farmer handed each girl a pitchfork and set a creaking wheelbarrow in front of them. Then he left them to their task.

"*¡Qué horror!*" Rosa exclaimed, turning a full circle. She grasped a small crucifix hanging around her neck and began murmuring to herself.

"What are you doing?" Andi asked, heading toward an empty stall. "Praying?"

"*Sí,*" came Rosa's fervent reply. "I'm praying this old barn holds together. Let's finish quickly and get out of here."

Andi smiled. "I'd much rather muck out stalls in this nice, cool barn than pick beans out in the sun." She threw a forkful of soiled hay into the wheelbarrow. "I've never worked so hard in my entire life as I have these past few days. I'll sure be glad when the bean harvest is over."

"Why? Do you think picking lettuce or melons or tomatoes will be easier?" Rosa asked, struggling with her pitchfork.

"You don't mean . . . ?" Andi paused at Rosa's slowly nodding head.

"If *Papá* cannot find steady work, we'll have to follow the crops all season in order to earn enough to live," she explained.

Andi leaned on the pitchfork and stared thoughtfully into the dirty stall. This was not the way she'd imagined things would turn out when she'd begged the Garduño family to allow her to stay with them. She'd been confident that she would find Taffy in a day or two and be on her way home by now.

Instead, Andi had discovered that searching for her horse could only be done in snatches, while passing through small, valley towns on the way to another harvesting job. The rest of her days were taken up with working, English lessons with the Garduños, and resting her sore and tired body.

"You want to go home, don't you?"

Rosa's question jerked Andi from her thoughts. She pitched another load of soiled hay into the wheelbarrow before tossing the pitchfork to the ground.

Go home? *Oh, if I only could!*

"I sure do," Andi said aloud. She picked a few pieces of hay from the skirt and blouse Nila had supplied. The Garduño family had been kind, but these weren't *her* clothes. It didn't feel right to wear them. "I . . . I miss my family."

Loneliness washed over Andi. "I miss curling up on my sister's bed and giggling over the funny things she tells me about her gentleman callers," she said. "I miss being invited to sit on the bunkhouse porch and listen to the cowhands' stories of the places they've been. I . . . I miss saying good night to my mother," she finished in a rush of words.

I even miss Chad's bossing, Andi admitted silently. She lifted the handles of the wheelbarrow and gave it a shove. It bumped and creaked toward the barn's open doors.

Rosa set aside her pitchfork. "*Papá* would take you home if you asked." She brushed a wayward strand of black hair from her face and followed Andi. "He's wanted to all along."

"I know." Andi dumped the heavy load just outside the door. "But I have to find my horse first."

Do you? a little voice inside her head mocked. *Do you really?*

"Did you learn anything yesterday in that town we passed through?" Rosa asked.

"Not a thing. I asked every person I met. I described Taffy's saddle and bridle, but nobody had seen her *or* that dirty, rotten, good-for-nothing horse thief who ran off with her." Andi mumbled the last part in angry English.

Rosa gaped at her.

"Don't worry," Andi assured her. "I'm not saying anything *really* awful. I just can't think of anything bad enough to call him in Spanish."

Rosa nodded and helped bring the wheelbarrow back into the barn for the second stall. "I could. I could teach you many bad things to call him, but I'd better not."

Andi let out a long, thoughtful breath. "You know what, Rosa? Looking for Taffy is turning out to be a harder job than I figured. That thief could be clear to Nevada by now." She thrust the pitchfork into a pile of soiled bedding. Then she paused.

"I wonder what Chad would say if I showed up at the ranch

without Taffy," she mused. For a moment, Rosa and the dirty stalls vanished, replaced by a vision of trudging up the driveway and seeing the ranch house. Mother waiting on the porch. Justin hugging her. Then Chad . . .

Andi imagined the devastated look on his face when she told him about Taffy. She cringed. "I can't. Not without Taffy." She gave her friend a pleading look. "Right?"

Rosa shook her head. "*No, mi amiga.* You should not be working like a *peón* in the fields. You need to go home." She grasped Andi's shoulders. "Think about it."

Andi slumped. "Maybe you're right." She nodded. "I'll think on it."

Ⓒ

Late that night, Andi lay curled up beside Rosa on a mound of old quilts. She was exhausted from another long, hot day in the fields, but she couldn't settle down to sleep. Her body ached. Her face burned from too much sun. She felt sticky with dried sweat.

Although Andi would never insult the Garduño family by saying anything, she couldn't deny the fact that she was hungry. She'd worked today for a bowl of rabbit stew and a piece of cornbread that had not filled her up. The beans and tortillas she'd so eagerly devoured that first day had become tiresome after a week. Worse, the portions had grown smaller.

Andi's stomach growled. *I'd give just about anything for a warm bath and a plate piled high with roast beef and potatoes and gravy.* Her mouth watered at the thought of a tall glass of cold milk and one of her mother's sugar cookies.

Rosa's words came back: *"You need to go home."*

Andi tossed and turned. Her thoughts buzzed like a swarm of angry bees as she considered her friend's pleading. Go home? Sleep in her own bed instead of on this hard ground? Go fishing next

Saturday instead of bending over an endless row of beans? Ride like the wind across acres and acres of—

No!

Andi's thoughts came to a screeching halt. There was nothing to ride *on*. If she went home now, she would have to admit to herself that Taffy was beyond reach. She'd have to face her brother with that truth, and she wasn't sure she could do it.

Chad was bossy—so determined, it seemed, to keep her from having a good time—but she loved him. She knew Taffy's loss would hurt him deeply. After all, Taffy had been his idea, his gift to Andi on her sixth birthday.

She had been astonished when Chad ripped off her bedcovers and spirited her away to the barn that spring morning nearly six years ago. Was it another one of his mean, teasing tricks? He seldom passed up an opportunity to annoy her, and she was just as often ready to challenge him back.

Yet there'd been no teasing in his bright blue eyes when he'd carefully set Andi down beside the wobbly-legged, golden filly. He had grinned at her surprised gasp and gently whispered, "Happy birthday, little sister."

Andi had stood frozen. A horse of her very own? She couldn't breathe. She didn't even blink for fear of spoiling that magic moment.

Finally, she reached out a hesitant finger and touched the filly's soft nose. The little one had sniffed the hand, jerked her head up, and scurried to the other side of a stately, white mare. A few seconds later, the foal had poked her head out from behind her mother and stared at Andi.

"Really, Chad? She's really, truly for me? You're not teasing?"

"You bet she's yours. I'm going to teach you how to gentle her and make her your friend. You'll have one fine filly when we're finished. I promise."

Chad had kept his promise. The countless hours he'd spent with

Andi and her filly had brought the three of them together in a special bond. In Andi's eyes, Taffy belonged to Chad as much as to her. Tears pooled in her eyes at the memory. She wouldn't go home without Taffy.

She didn't dare.

Andi lay still and gazed up into a sky awash with stars. Her decision to keep searching made her feel lonelier than ever. What was her family doing right now? Were they looking for her? What about Taffy? Where was her horse? Did the drifter still have her? Was she frightened or mistreated?

Andi sniffed back her tears and offered up a quiet prayer for her family and her best friend. *I know I don't deserve any favors, Lord, but please help me find Taffy. Not for myself, but so I can take her home, where she'll be safe.*

Then she rolled over and fell asleep as dawn began to fill the sky.

Chapter Eight

A CLUE

Not much of a town, Andi decided after her first glimpse of Livingston Flats. She stood with the Garduño family at the edge of town and gazed down Main Street.

A couple dozen drab, flimsy wooden buildings with false fronts lined the dusty street on either side. The signs for a bank, a hotel, three saloons, and a general store caught her attention. She imagined the rest of the buildings held similar businesses. At the very end of the street, Andi could make out the railroad depot.

In a town this small and run-down, she thought with a glimmer of hope, *Taffy should stand out like a gold nugget in a gravel bed. Someone will certainly remember seeing her. All I have to do is find the right person.*

"I'm going to ask around and see if anyone's seen Taffy," Andi told Nila.

The woman nodded. "José does not need you to speak for us now. Perhaps later." She indicated her husband, who had moved away to join a few of his countrymen in front of a small cantina.

"May I come with you?" Rosa asked. "I'd like to help look for your horse."

"Of course." Andi held out her hand. "It would be nice to have a friend along."

Smiling, Rosa grasped Andi's hand, and the two girls headed down the street.

"We'll walk through town and ask anyone who happens along," Andi said, skipping across the street. She was in high spirits at the possibility of learning something about Taffy this afternoon.

The door to the two-story hotel opened, and a smartly dressed couple stepped out. Andi greeted them with a cheerful smile. "Excuse me. Have you seen a golden palomino horse with a—"

The man pulled his companion closer to his side and brushed past Andi. The couple hurried along the boardwalk and disappeared into the bank without a backward glance.

Andi stared after the couple. "They sure weren't very friendly. I wonder why." She grabbed Rosa's arm and pointed down the street. "Let's try the general store. Lots of folks are going in and out."

Andi stood outside the entrance and talked to a dozen shoppers before she realized she wasn't getting anywhere. Most of the women wouldn't speak to her. Those who replied to her questions did so in short, clipped sentences before hurrying away.

"I don't understand it." Andi folded her arms across her chest. "Of all the rude, sour folks I've ever met, the people of this town take the prize."

Rosa shrugged. "Your hair is dark and you're dressed like me, so they think you're a Mexican."

Andi glanced down at the skirt and blouse. Her cheeks grew hot in sudden understanding. She looked up at her friend and opened her mouth. No words came out.

"*Lo siento,*" Rosa murmured.

Andi shook her head. "No. *I'm* the one who's sorry. Sorry some folks have to act so uppity." She squeezed Rosa's hand. "Come on. Let's not let their bad manners spoil our day."

The two girls continued down the street. They passed the newspaper office, a millinery shop, and a doctor's small office without meeting anyone. Andi was ready to give up and return to the Garduño family camp when a young cowhand came out of the telegraph office and began to untie his horse.

"Hey, mister," Andi called out. "Can I ask you something?"

He looked up. "Sure, missy." He leaned against his horse in an easy manner and pushed his wide-brimmed hat away from his forehead. "Shoot."

At last! A friendly fellow! "Have you seen a golden palomino mare around these parts?"

The man lost his grin and straightened up. He frowned in thought. "I might've," he said. "Describe her."

"She's just under fifteen hands high, with a white blaze on her nose and four white socks. Her mane and tail are creamy white."

The cowhand looked thoughtful. "Anything else? Saddle? Brand?"

Andi nodded and dropped to her knees. With her finger, she traced a large letter C in the dusty street. Then she drew a circle around the C. "This is our brand, the Circle C." She dusted off her hands and rose to her feet. "The saddle is decorated with fancy etchings and silver conchos."

The man nodded at Andi's recital. "I've seen a horse like that—just last week, in fact." He whistled appreciatively. "A right pretty little filly . . . and impressive tack."

"Here? In Livingston Flats?" Andi couldn't believe her good fortune. A clue at last! "Where did you see her?"

"Well . . ." He shuffled uncomfortably and glanced over his shoulder.

Andi followed his gaze. Across the street, a sign advertising Jake's Place hung above a larger sign that read Saloon. "Go on," she insisted.

The cowhand turned to face her. "Why are you asking all these questions?"

"My horse was stolen two weeks ago. I've been looking for her everywhere."

"Well, missy," he said, "I don't have good news for you." He pointed to the saloon. "A fella rode into town on a palomino like the one you described and lost her in a card game a few hours later." He shook his head. "I only remember the incident cuz he practically tore the place apart when he lost all his money. The whole town couldn't help but hear the ruckus. Sheriff tossed him in jail to shut him up."

"What about my horse?" Andi persisted. She didn't want to hear about that miserable horse thief.

"I don't know the fella who won her," the man continued. "He wasn't a local. I reckon he was just passing through town. He mounted his own horse and led the palomino away. Haven't seen either of them since." He paused. "Have you checked with the sheriff?"

Andi shook her head. She wasn't eager to involve a sheriff in her search. A sheriff was bound to ask questions she'd prefer not to answer.

The cowhand shrugged. "Sheriff probably couldn't help you, anyhow. The fella who won your horse is most likely long gone." He pointed down the street. "You might try the livery stable. Jon March knows just about everything that goes on in this town. Who knows? He might've boarded your horse for the night. Perhaps he even bought her. He's quite the horse trader."

"The livery stable," Andi repeated, nodding. "Yes, I'll check there." She smiled at the young man. "Thank you, mister."

"My pleasure, missy." He tipped his hat to Andi, nodded at Rosa, and mounted his horse. "A word of advice. Jon March can be downright unpleasant at times. Watch yourselves."

Before she could respond, the cowhand rode away.

Andi shared the cowhand's story in Spanish with Rosa then raised a hand to shade her eyes from the sun. She scanned the street. "I see the livery stable. It's just a couple blocks away. Let's go."

The girls hurried along the boardwalk and crossed the street to a large, dilapidated building with a faded sign proclaiming March's Livery Stable & Feed. An enormous set of double doors hung open, allowing light to penetrate the dim interior.

A smaller door to the left of the stables opened, and a heavily built, scruffy-looking man emerged from the shadows. When he saw the girls, he planted his meaty fists on his hips and scowled.

"Are you Mr. Jon March?" Andi asked.

The man gave Andi a curt nod and pulled a pipe from between clenched teeth. "I ain't got no jobs for hire," he declared. "And I don't rent to your kind."

Andi frowned at the man's rudeness. "I'm not looking for a job, and I don't want to rent your horses."

"That so?" He thrust the pipe back into his mouth. He eyed the girls suspiciously. "Then what's your business?"

"I'm looking for a horse you might have boarded here a week or two ago. A golden palomino mare."

The man's eyes widened, and Andi paused. Then he cleared his throat. "Nope. Haven't boarded nothin' like that. Now, get outta here."

"But I've barely described her." Andi took a determined step forward. "If you'd let me finish, maybe you'd remember—"

"No!" Mr. March said between clenched teeth. He closed the distance between himself and the girls and pulled the pipe from his mouth. His hand shook as he jabbed the stem toward Andi. "Listen, girl, and listen good. I haven't boarded the horse you're describing. Not last week. Not any week."

"May I look inside your stable?" Andi asked.

"No," he snapped. "This here's private property." His eyes narrowed as he looked over the girls' shoulders. "I got a customer. Go on now. Get off my place."

Andi didn't move. "Someone won her in a card game. She was wearing an expensive saddle."

The owner shoved his dirty, unkempt face into Andi's, causing her to stagger backward. He caught her and pulled her to her feet. In a low, harsh voice he growled, "I told you I don't know nothin' about a palomino. Now clear outta here and don't come back. If I see you near my place again, I'll have the law on you. Understand?"

Andi nodded and shook herself free of the man's grip.

Mr. March brushed past the two girls. He hailed his customer with a friendly wave of his pipe. "George! Howdy! You here for a rig? Come on in the office and we'll talk."

Andi watched the two men disappear through the small door and into the shadows. Then she fixed her gaze on the large, open doors leading to the stables. "Come on, Rosa." She tugged on her friend's sleeve.

"What's happening?" Rosa wanted to know. "I didn't understand any of that."

"The owner acts like he's hiding something," Andi explained. She led her friend around to the side of the livery. "He wouldn't listen to me. He wouldn't even let me look at his horses. He seemed jumpy and mighty anxious for us to leave."

She peeked around the corner. Mr. March and his customer were leaving the office. They headed toward a nearby lean-to, where an assortment of different sized buggies waited to be rented. "Maybe he's got Taffy in the stable. I'm going to find out."

As soon as the two men were out of sight, Andi sprinted across the yard and ducked into the livery stable's gaping blackness. She beckoned to Rosa, who crept up beside her and looked around.

"Another rickety barn." Rosa shook her head.

Andi shushed her and headed for the horses. There were a dozen stalls, most of them occupied. When her eyes adjusted to the poor light, Andi began her search. She poked her head into each stall, talking softly to avoid startling the horses. Rosa followed close behind.

Finally, Andi reached the end of the stalls and stopped. "Taffy's not here. I was so sure that man was hiding something." She leaned against the back wall and gazed down the aisle, lost in thought.

Rosa's worried voice brought Andi back. "Let's leave before he returns and finds us here."

Andi made her way toward the light, sick at heart. *Oh, Taffy! Where are you? I was so close! What do I do now?*

Not wanting to overlook any detail, however small, she crossed the open area in front of the doors and explored the other side of the livery stable. This part of the building was piled high with things needed to run the livery: hay, sacks of feed, horse tack, harnesses, spare wheels, buggy whips, tools, and saddle blankets. There were even a number of old saddlebags and canteens heaped in a corner.

Andi carefully picked through the worn and ill-kept items. She lifted aside the blankets, peeked behind a stack of empty wooden crates, and examined the sorry assortment of saddles. Then she knelt in the corner and began digging through the clutter of saddlebags and canteens.

"What are you looking for?" Rosa whispered, glancing nervously toward the open doors.

"A clue. Anything to prove Taffy was here." Andi tossed a canteen to the side and sighed in defeat. "But it looks like this is another dead end." She stood up and gave the pile of goods a frustrated kick. One set of saddlebags went flying and landed with a thud beside Rosa.

Andi spared it a careless glance before turning to leave. Disappointment crushed her. *Where do I go from here?* She reached down to toss the bags back onto the pile then frowned. Her heart skipped a beat. "Rosa!" she exclaimed in a low whisper. "I think I found something."

Andi dropped to her knees and pulled her friend down beside her. With shaking hands, she turned the saddlebags over and pointed. "Look!" Carved along the edge of the flap were the letters AC. "My initials."

She lifted the flap and groped inside. Empty. Quickly, desperately, Andi grabbed the other saddlebag and reached inside. Her fingers closed around something hard and crusty—an old, dry chunk of bread. Ugh! She tossed it aside and kept digging.

This time her search brought a reward. She pulled out a smooth, stiff piece of paper and caught her breath. A photograph. Half of it had been ripped away, as if the searchers had seen it and tried to discard it.

She blinked back tears. "It's my family."

Rosa scooted closer and looked over Andi's shoulder. *"Qué familia hermosa,"* she whispered.

Andi studied each face. *Yes, I do have a beautiful family.* Guilt for leaving home washed over her. *I wish I—*

"Is there anything else in the bag?" Rosa wanted to know.

Andi stuffed the torn photo inside the waistband of her skirt and opened wide the saddlebag. "I don't think so." She paused and peered closer. "Wait a minute. There *is* something more." She drew out three small coins. "Thirty cents."

Rosa's eyes widened. "We're rich."

Chapter Nine

A DIME'S WORTH OF TROUBLE

Andi slung the saddlebags over her shoulder and stood up. "Come on, Rosa, let's get out of here."

"You're not taking those things with you, are you?"

"Why not? They're mine." Andi took a few steps toward the exit and froze. Boisterous laughter and men's voices filtered through the livery stable's thin walls.

Jon March was returning.

"Maybe you're right, Rosa." Andi dropped the saddlebags where she stood. Frantically, she searched the shadows for another way out of the stable.

Nothing. No windows. No back door.

Rosa clutched her arm. "Let's hide!"

Andi nodded. As quietly as she could, she led Rosa through the maze of cast-off equipment, barrels of metal parts, and stacks of crates. She shuddered, imagining the livery owner's fury if he found them trespassing inside his barn.

"I'll get the horses and hitch up your rig. Won't take but a minute," Mr. March shouted. He entered the stable at a brisk walk.

Andi ducked behind a haystack, pulling Rosa beside her. She flattened herself against the prickly alfalfa and held her breath. *Please don't let him find us*, she prayed. Her heart raced out of control.

What seemed like an eternity later, Andi peeked around the hay and watched Mr. March lead two bay horses outside. She let out a sigh of relief and tapped her friend on the shoulder. "Let's go," she mouthed in Spanish.

Without a sound, the two girls crept from their hiding place and darted through the open doors into the sunshine. They didn't stop running until they reached the general store three blocks away.

"I think we got away." Andi drew in huge gulps of air. "Let's rest." She threw herself onto a crude wooden bench in front of the store and leaned her head back against the large glass window, breathing deeply. "That was close."

"*Sí,*" Rosa agreed. "But I am sorry you did not find your horse."

"She was *here*, Rosa. That's something. I'm getting closer." Andi glanced toward the store's open doorway. "Why don't we go inside and look around? We've got thirty cents, you know."

"Should we spend so much money, *amiga*?"

Andi bit her lip. The Garduño family had very little money, certainly not enough to spend on a foolish whim. She should really turn the money over to José, who would use it to buy the things his family so desperately needed. *Still . . .*

"Is there anything you ever wanted to buy for yourself, if you had a few pennies of your own?"

Rosa stared at Andi. Then she ducked her head and nodded shyly. "*Sí.*" She pulled her long, black braid over her shoulder. "I have always wanted a ribbon for my hair. A red ribbon." She twirled her braid and sighed wistfully.

Andi pulled a dime from her skirt pocket. "We can easily buy a red ribbon with this dime and have plenty left over for a fistful of licorice besides. I'll give the other twenty cents to your father." She stood up and beckoned Rosa. "Come on."

When they entered the store, Andi nudged her friend. "It's time to practice the English I've taught you this past week."

Rosa turned pale. "*No estoy lista.*"

"Sure you're ready!" Andi said in English. She held out a spool of red satin ribbon. "You go up to the shopkeeper and say, 'I would like one yard of ribbon.' Then we'll pick out the licorice. Here. Take it."

Rosa took the spool with a shaky hand. Andi followed her to the counter, prodding her in the back several times when the girl stalled in fear.

"You can do it," Andi whispered in her ear when they reached the counter.

The shopkeeper was a round-faced man with a balding head and a handlebar mustache. Tufts of hair stuck out over his ears. He greeted Andi and Rosa with a friendly smile. "What'll it be, girls?"

Rosa swallowed and set the spool of ribbon on the counter. "I like . . . *would* like . . ." She faltered. Andi nudged her. Rosa began again. "I would like one yard ribb—"

"Stand aside."

A tall, brown-haired girl interrupted Rosa. She and another fashionably dressed young lady squeezed their way between Andi and Rosa, shoving them apart.

"Mr. Martin, I need these things right away," the tall girl demanded in a voice clearly used to being obeyed. She pushed a slip of paper across the counter. "My father is expecting me home soon. Fill this order immediately." She waved a careless hand at Andi. "Get away from here. Both of you. You can wait outside until I'm finished."

Andi didn't move.

"Oh, Felicity!" Her blond companion giggled. "They probably don't speak English."

Andi's stomach knotted at Felicity's rudeness. The temper that so often got her into trouble at home threatened to boil over. "I *do* speak English."

She snatched the ribbon from a bewildered-looking Rosa, slammed it down on the counter, and carefully laid her dime next to it. "One yard of ribbon, please." She locked gazes with the storekeeper. "And five sticks of licorice."

Felicity's companion gasped at Andi's boldness.

Mr. Martin shook his head and gave his attention to an obviously furious Felicity. "I'll prepare your order right away, Miss Felicity."

Andi watched in stunned silence while Mr. Martin bustled around the store. He wrapped the girl's order in brown paper and tied it up with a piece of string. "That will be a dollar and fifteen cents."

Felicity leaned across the counter to press the coins into the shopkeeper's hand. "You would do well to be extra careful, Mr. Martin," she confided in a low voice. "Those kind will steal you blind when your back's turned." She gave Andi a scornful look. Then, with a flounce of her skirt, she linked arms with her friend and strutted out of the store.

Andi's cheeks burned like she'd been slapped. She didn't care about Rosa's English lesson any longer. She didn't care about the red ribbon. This storekeeper clearly did not want Andi's business, not after setting her and Rosa aside in favor of that uppity young lady.

She shoved the spool toward Mr. Martin. "I don't want this ribbon after all, mister." She had a sudden, terrible urge to chase after the girl named Felicity and slap her.

The shopkeeper nodded, as if he could read Andi's thoughts. "I understand, and I'm sorry. Miss Felicity can be . . . difficult." He cut a length of ribbon and handed it to her. "No charge. Please accept my apologies."

Andi took the ribbon with a nod of thanks. She gave it to Rosa and whispered, "I've had a bellyful of this town. I'm *glad* Taffy's not here any longer. Let's find your parents and leave this place."

In a town the size of Livingston Flats, it didn't take long to find the Garduño family. They stood right where Andi had left them earlier in the day, near the edge of town. Nila waited quietly, watching the farm wagons and townsfolk pass by. Joselito was scratching behind the burro's ears, murmuring to the small beast as it stood harnessed to the wagon. A few yards beyond the group, José appeared in earnest conversation with a countryman.

Andi perched herself on the side of the wagon to listen.

"Listen, *amigo*," José was saying. "My family is looking for steady work. Have you heard of anything around these parts?"

Andi wondered how many times José had asked that question this afternoon. By the look of desperation on his face, she guessed it was a lot. For their sakes, Andi hoped the Garduños could find a job. Their supplies were getting alarmingly low, and Andi knew the thirty cents she planned to give José wouldn't buy more than a few pounds of beans.

Andi had an uneasy feeling that if they didn't get a job soon, she would be forced to admit defeat and go home. José certainly couldn't afford to feed an extra mouth much longer.

"Depends on how particular you are, *amigo*," the other man answered with a thoughtful frown.

"We're not particular," José said. He waved toward the wagon. "My family and I will do anything. Even a steady harvesting job would be welcome—one where we can stay in one place for longer than a few days."

Andi cringed. *Please! No beans*, she begged silently. Anything but backbreaking harvest work.

"Speak any English?"

"Not much," José admitted. "But there are some in my family who do." He glanced at Andi.

"Well . . ." The man scratched his chin and shook his head, as if unwilling to offer more information.

"Tell me," José insisted.

"There might be work out at the Lazy L ranch."

"What kind of work?"

The man snorted. "Hard work."

"Could you tell me more, maybe?" José asked.

"I could, I guess, but you might be sorry. The Lazy L is not the

73

best place to work. The *ranchero, Señor* Livingston, pays well, but he is a hard taskmaster and difficult to please. Especially if you're Mexican."

Andi watched José digest the man's advice. He didn't seem concerned about the working conditions. The words "pays well" had made his whole face light up.

"What work?" José persisted.

"They are in need of a cleaning woman. The last one couldn't get along with the housekeeper. She's an old woman who's run the place for years. If you can't get along with *Señora* Nelson, you're out."

"My wife could clean," José murmured.

"They always need harvest hands," the man went on. "The foreman out there isn't too bad for a *gringo*."

José grinned. "I must go there at once before others seek out the positions." He took a step toward his family. "Wife! We are—"

"There is no rush." The man tugged on José's arm. "Livingston Flats is a slow-moving town. They haven't had a cleaning woman up at the house for a couple of weeks. I wouldn't let *my* wife work there."

"Perhaps your wife is not as hungry as mine."

The man laughed. "That may be so, *amigo*." He gave José a friendly slap on the shoulder. "There is also a job for a girl who can speak some English. A pair of young legs to fetch and carry for the *señorita* and the housekeeper. The last girl was thrown out a week ago."

"Why?" José inquired.

"They say she was caught with one of the *señorita*'s handkerchiefs. A small thing, to be sure, but the *señorita* was enraged. They say she is even harder to please than her father." He shrugged. "No one stays long on the Lazy L. You will find this out for yourself if you go there. Still, you asked me if I knew of a place that would hire you, and I have told you what I know."

José nodded. "*Gracias*. I am grateful for all you have told me. Could you give me directions to this *rancho*?"

"*Sí.*"

José stayed in high spirits all the way back to their small camp. "We shall make such an impression on the Livingstons that he cannot help but hire the Garduño family. We will work hard, mind our own business, and give this *ranchero* no call to find fault with us or our people."

He waved toward a small, bubbling creek. "There is water. Wash yourselves. Wash your clothes. Tomorrow morning we go to the Lazy L!"

Chapter Ten

THE LAZY L RANCH

The next morning, Andi found herself standing with the Garduño family on the porch of the Lazy L, waiting for someone to answer the door. Just glancing around this fine-looking ranch—the two-story white house with freshly painted green shutters, the well-kept barns and outbuildings, the acres of irrigated pastureland—made Andi's heart squeeze with homesickness. Her resolve to keep searching for Taffy was again being tested.

She swallowed the lump in her throat and stared at the porch swing. *A few more days*, she thought. *I can hold out for a few more days. I'll ask the cowhands here about Taffy. Maybe they know something the livery stable owner wouldn't tell me.*

The front door opened, and Andi jumped in surprise. A tall, silver-haired woman scowled at them. She tapped her foot impatiently. "Yes? What do you want?"

Andi winced. The woman's Spanish was terrible. How would they ever understand her?

José removed his *sombrero* and bowed. "We are the Garduño family. I heard in town that you are in need of a cleaning woman."

The woman gave a curt nod. "Yes. That's true." She eyed each member of the family carefully, as if her piercing gaze would uncover any dark secrets. Apparently satisfied, she said, "I am Mrs. Nelson, the housekeeper. I'm worn out trying to keep this place in order.

Mr. Livingston has instructed me to find a replacement as soon as possible." She motioned to Nila. "You may work for a few days. Then we shall see."

Nila's face lit up. *"Gracias, señora."*

"What about the others?" Mrs. Nelson asked.

"My son and I hope to work in the fields," José replied. "And my . . . *daughters* . . ." He cleared his throat and flicked a nervous glance at Andi. "Perhaps you need young servants who are light and quick on their feet to run errands for you? Both girls are used to hard work."

I am now, Andi added with a quiet sigh.

"These girls look too young," Mrs. Nelson said with a frown.

"That may be true, but Andrea speaks English." He prodded her forward. "You are looking for such a one, *no?* To wait on the *señorita?"*

"Is this true?" Mrs. Nelson asked in English, giving Andi a hard look. "You speak English?"

Andi smiled. "Yes, ma'am." It was such a relief to hear words from the housekeeper that didn't sound cracked or broken.

"Humph," Mrs. Nelson snorted. "A Mexican speaking decent English. I should live to see the day." Her gaze met Andi's and held it. "You might do as a maid to Miss Livingston, in addition to other duties, of course. But understand this: being a maid for the young mistress of this house is an important position. She was displeased with the last girl. Your English must be better than what she's put up with in the past. What do you have to say?"

"She won't be disappointed," Andi answered. "I can understand anything she says."

Mrs. Nelson's gray eyes opened wide listening to Andi's reply. A small smile cracked her face, and her voice took on a slight warmth. "Very good." She nodded at Nila. "I will allow your daughters to take the positions on a trial basis." She turned to José. "Talk to Clem, the foreman. He will find you work, and he speaks Spanish."

"Gracias, señora. Muchas gracias." José bowed.

Mrs. Nelson turned her back on José and waved Nila and the girls into the house. "Mr. Livingston is giving an important dinner party tonight. Everything must be spotless. You have arrived at the Lazy L at a good time."

She led her new help into the kitchen then turned and regarded them with a critical eye. "This is a proud home, and I will have no one disgracing it. The servants who work here are quiet, submissive, and quickly obedient to Mr. Livingston, his daughter, and to me. Do you understand?"

Barely, Andi confessed silently. She wished Mrs. Nelson would speak English. Nila and Rosa looked confused, but they nodded at the housekeeper's words.

"Good." Mrs. Nelson brought out a tarnished silver tea service and placed it on the large worktable in the center of the kitchen. "You two," she told Nila and Rosa, "get to work polishing the silver." She glanced at Andi. "You, come with me."

Andi followed the housekeeper into the dining room, where the woman waved an arm to indicate the table. "Your task, Andrea," she explained in English, "will be to set this table for the evening meal. There will be eight people in all, and it will be a formal dinner. Have you ever seen a table set formally?"

"Yes."

Mrs. Nelson's eyebrows shot up. "Indeed? We'll see about that. The last girl didn't know the difference between a salad fork and a spoon."

Andi made no reply.

"All right, child, let's see what you can do. Set the table immediately. When you finish, we'll see about meeting your new mistress."

"You want me to set the table for a dinner party at ten o'clock in the morning?" Andi asked, astonished.

Mrs. Nelson turned around and glared at her. "I want instant obedience without foolish questions."

Andi gulped back her surprise. "Yes, ma'am."

The housekeeper left the room.

Setting the table was not her favorite task at home, so Andi had learned to do it quickly and correctly. In a short time the plates, knives, forks, spoons, glasses, and napkins were in their proper positions. She gave the table a final, satisfied glance before hurrying back to the kitchen. Mrs. Nelson would not find any fault with her work.

Nila and Rosa were still busy at their task of polishing the tea set. Mother and daughter chatted, clearly happy to be inside this fine home rather than outside picking beans under a hot sun.

Andi took a seat next to her friends. "I like polishing silver. Do you need some help?"

When Nila nodded, Andi picked up a rag and the silver polish. "When my sister Melinda and I polish the silver together, we have a grand time. She tells me the funniest stories about the young men who come calling on her."

She grinned at the memory, forgetting for a moment her intention to keep her origins a secret from the Garduños. "Once when Jeffrey Sullivan was trying to impress her, he fell backward, right into the horse trough. Wish I'd been there to see it. I would've pushed him in myself. He thinks he's so smart!"

Rosa giggled. "You would really do such a thing?"

"Sure I would. Jeffrey needs a good dunking now and again. He's so moonstruck over Melinda, he can't see straight. My brother Mitch says cold water is just the thing to cool Jeffrey off and bring him to his senses. Mitch told me the next time I want to play a trick on Jeffrey I should . . ." She paused and glanced down at the rag in her hand, lost in thought. Her smile faded.

"You should do what?" Rosa urged, clearly enjoying this amusing story of Andi's family. "What trick?"

"N-nothing." Andi rubbed hard on the silver.

An uncomfortable silence fell.

"You miss your family, don't you?" Nila asked gently.

More than I ever thought I would. Andi put down the silver sugar bowl and sighed. "*Sí, señora.* I'd give anything to go home right now." Then she set her jaw. "But what I want doesn't count. I can't go home until I find my horse."

"It is only a horse."

"No. I told you how it is. I've done everything wrong. Everything! I can't face my brother without Taffy."

"Can't," Nila asked, "or *won't*?" When Andi didn't answer, she continued. "Are you sure it's not your own stubborn pride that's keeping you from going home? If you think about it for one minute, *chiquita*, you'll realize your family is only interested in finding *you*, not your horse. You have been gone a long time."

Andi turned her head away so Nila could not see the tears welling up in her eyes. She picked up the cream pitcher and polished furiously.

Mrs. Nelson entered the kitchen just then, preventing any further conversation. She reached out and grabbed Andi by the arm. The cream pitcher clattered to the floor. "How dare you disobey me!" she scolded in English. "This is not your job. Go back at once and finish the table."

Andi bent down and picked up the pitcher. She placed it in the housekeeper's outstretched hand. "The table is all set, Mrs. Nelson."

"We'll see about that," the housekeeper snapped. She beckoned Andi to follow.

When they entered the dining room, the expression on Mrs. Nelson's face turned from annoyance to joy. She clasped her hands together and favored Andi with a rare smile. "Very good, Andrea. Very good indeed. You may be a girl I can work with, after all."

"Thank you. Now, may I go back and help with the silver?"

Mrs. Nelson took a deep breath. "I'm afraid not. You must come with me. It's time to meet your new mistress."

Chapter Eleven

ANDI'S NEW JOB

I told the young miss I found her a new maid," Mrs. Nelson explained, leading Andi through the Livingston house. "She wasn't pleased with the news. She has her own ideas of what a maid should be. So far, neither her father nor I have been able to find one to satisfy her."

Andi bit back a reply. She knew good and well Mrs. Nelson would not want the new servant girl's thoughts on the subject. She followed the housekeeper up a long flight of stairs, down a wide hallway, and into a lavish room full of ruffles and lace.

Andi's eyes opened wide. Like discarded rags, yards and yards of satin and fine silk lay strewn across the mahogany four-poster bed. An enormous trunk rested on its side in the middle of the room, the contents spilling onto the floor in disarray. Across the room, next to an open wardrobe, stood a mahogany bureau. Every drawer was open. Most of the clothes had been tossed onto the floor to join the rest of the clutter. A dozen or so carelessly stacked dishes rested atop the dresser, giving the room a final touch of disorder and chaos.

"I haven't time to keep her room looking nice these days," Mrs. Nelson whispered. "That will be your job."

No wonder she can't keep a maid, Andi thought in distaste. Her heart sank at the size of this new task.

A sudden scuffling noise on the other side of the bed caught Andi's attention.

Mrs. Nelson jammed her hands on her hips. "What are you up to now, miss?"

"I . . . can't . . . find it!" A high, screechy voice came from under the bed.

The next instant, amidst a great deal of banging and complaining, a girl about Melinda's age rose from the floor and peered over the top of the bed. Her cheeks were flushed, and her fine, brown hair tumbled around her narrow face in wild curls. Her hazel eyes flashed with annoyance. "I've looked everywhere!"

"That's obvious," Mrs. Nelson observed dryly. She pushed Andi forward. "I found a girl to see to your needs and keep your room straightened. Andrea, meet Miss Felicity Livingston."

For one horrible moment, Andi thought she was going to be sick. Her palms grew sweaty, and her heart leaped to her throat. She swallowed. "We've met."

Felicity straightened, shook out her riding skirt, and frowned. "What do you mean? Where could I have possibly met *you*?" She wrinkled her nose.

Andi held the older girl's haughty look. "Yesterday. At the general store."

Felicity's mouth dropped open. Then her face broke into a satisfied smile. She chuckled. "Indeed, we have met." Her eyes gleamed with interest. "For once, Agatha, you might have found me a housemaid I can work with. The last girl was a silly, empty-headed little thing. I couldn't get her to do anything I told her. Her only English words were *yes, miss* and *no, miss*."

Mrs. Nelson pursed her lips at Felicity's comments. "As you can see, this girl speaks English quite well."

Felicity grunted. "So she does." She picked up a dress from her bed and tossed it to Mrs. Nelson. "I want this for the dinner party tonight. Make sure each of the pleats on the underskirt is properly pressed." She waved the housekeeper away. "That will be all. I want to instruct my new maid in her duties."

"As you wish." Mrs. Nelson gathered up the yards of fabric and left the room.

Felicity hurried around the bed. She lifted one of Andi's thick, dark braids and gazed into her face. "I remember you. I also remember how you spoke out of turn and tried to get Mr. Martin to help you. You should have stood aside and allowed me to go first, which is the proper thing to do. You are an impudent girl and need to learn your place." She smirked. "I shall be more than happy to instruct you."

Dread swept through Andi. *I bet you will.*

Felicity frowned and let Andi's braid fall back into place. "I guess you'll do. You're not as bad looking as the last girl. In fact, you're kind of cute—as far as servant girls go. I do hope you're as quick on your feet as you are with your tongue." She laughed. "And at least you don't stink."

Andi's cheeks burned at the comment. Her hand itched to slap the girl's sneering face. *I can't hit her. I can't.* She kept her fists at her sides.

"You will do everything I say and always act respectfully toward me and my family," Felicity said. "Remember, you're in America now. If you don't like it, you can go back to Mexico. But while you're here, *I'm* the boss." She paused, as if expecting a response. "I'm speaking to you, girl."

"Yes, Miss Felicity." Andi swallowed her disgust with difficulty and forced her tightly clamped fingers to relax.

"Good. Now, your duties." Felicity waved her arm around her room. "My bed is to be made up daily and my room cleaned. You will set out my clothes for dinner and any special event. My riding clothes, especially, must be ready whenever I want them. You will bring breakfast up to my room at precisely nine o'clock each morning." She took a deep breath. "You won't be having any free time.

I can always find something for you to do. If nothing else, you can brush my horse."

"Yes, Miss Felicity." Andi looked at the floor.

"Now, girl, the first thing—"

"My name's Andrea."

Before Andi could blink, Felicity grabbed one of her braids and gave it a hard jerk, sending Andi to the floor. "You must *never* interrupt me. Is that clear? I won't stand for any of your sass."

Andi shot to her feet. Her scalp tingled. She took a step in Felicity's direction. "Don't pull my hair," she said between clenched teeth.

Felicity laughed. "I'll do what I like without your say-so." She tugged Andi's braid then crossed her arms. "So, you're one of those uppity servants, are you? You think because you speak English you're as good as Americans? You will learn your place around here very quickly." She indicated her room. "Get to work. I want this room cleaned up, my bed made, and these awful dishes removed. Later, I will need help dressing for dinner."

She paused. When Andi didn't reply, she tapped her foot. "Well?"

Andi gave the girl a curt nod.

"Answer me."

"Yes, Miss Felicity."

"I'm doing you a favor by allowing you to work for me, you know. If you displease me or give me any back talk, you'll feel the sting of my riding crop—if I ever find it." Her face contorted into an impatient scowl. She resumed her search for the missing item, ignoring Andi as one might ignore a fly.

"Is this what you're looking for?" Andi asked a few minutes later. She held up a long, wicked-looking riding whip. The ends were frayed, indicating much use.

Felicity snatched the crop from Andi's hand. "Where did you find it?"

"Right here on the window sill, leaning against the curtain."

"Now I can go riding," Felicity said with glee. She flicked her wrist. The whip whistled then connected with the bedpost with a loud *crack*.

Andi jumped at the noise. "You don't really hit your horse with that thing, do you?"

"Of course I do, you ignorant peasant. How else do you make a stubborn animal obey?" She lost her smile. "Right now I've an extra-willful horse on my hands. I plan on showing the beast who the real boss is." She left, slamming the door behind her.

Andi ran to the window and watched Felicity head for the large barn. The girl passed a corral where four fine-looking horses stood quietly. As soon as they saw Felicity, the horses bunched together and headed for the other side of the corral. Felicity raised her whip and brought it down across the top railing.

The horses scattered in a panic, whinnying and neighing their distress. Felicity disappeared into the barn.

"You did that on purpose just to frighten them," Andi shouted, knowing Felicity couldn't hear her.

She turned away from the window and made her way to Felicity's bed. Angry and aching inside, Andi sat down and looked around the room. The similarity between Felicity's room and her own bedroom back home hit her like a bolt of lightning. She felt not only a sharp pang of regret, but also a grim sense of justice. What she had sown in irresponsibility back home, she was now reaping in abundance.

Andi reached into her waistband and pulled out the torn and wrinkled photograph. "I'm sorry, Mother," she whispered to the woman in the picture. "I'll never, *never* think I'm being treated unfairly again—not so long as I live. Chad was right. I've been nothing but trouble lately."

She looked up at the ceiling. "I haven't obeyed You very well either, Lord, running away like I did. What was I *thinking*?" She stuffed the photograph back in her waistband. "I'm no better than Felicity."

Determined to make the best of a bad situation, Andi rose from the bed and began the unpleasant task of straightening Felicity's room. It wasn't easy and took the rest of the day. While she was sweeping up the final bit of dirt, Felicity entered and began to undress. She tossed her old clothes onto the freshly made bed.

"Is my dress pressed?" she demanded.

Andi nodded. "Mrs. Nelson hung it up a few minutes ago."

Felicity threw open her wardrobe doors and examined the dark green silk dinner dress. She ran her fingers along the cream-colored picot trim and nodded her approval. "First you must help me with my corset," she directed, tossing the undergarment onto the bed. "It must be laced just so."

Andi did what she was told. She tightened Felicity's corset and wondered for the hundredth time why anyone would want to wear something tight enough to make breathing difficult. Melinda had just recently begun wearing one, but only for special occasions. Andi intended to avoid this particular part of growing up for as long as she could.

"Now the hoops," Felicity commanded, breaking into Andi's thoughts. "And my petticoats. The train on this dress must rise in the back exactly right or it will look dreadful."

Yards and yards of rich, flowing fabric settled around the girl. She attached a piece of gathered lace to her throat and shook out her full overskirt. Felicity suddenly looked *years* older than Melinda.

"Here." Felicity handed Andi a brush. "One hundred strokes should be good enough." She sat down and picked up a book. "What are you waiting for? Start brushing."

Andi looked at the brush in her hand. Would this day never end? She began to brush the girl's long hair.

". . . ninety-eight . . . ninety-nine . . . one hundred." Andi tossed the brush onto the vanity. "All done."

"What? Are you sure you counted correctly? I've hardly finished this chapter."

"I count very well, Miss Felicity," Andi answered, an edge in her voice. She was tired and hungry. She'd been given no lunch and wondered when she could join the Garduño family for supper.

"Maybe not as well as you think. Here, take the brush and count out loud this time so I can hear you."

Andi had no choice but to begin anew. Her arm ached by the time she finished.

Felicity closed the book with a bang. "My goodness! Look at the time! You're as slow as molasses, girl. My dinner guests will be arriving any moment. You'd better learn to do things more quickly. Go on, now. Leave me alone." She turned toward her vanity, her fingers flying to arrange her hair.

Andi wearily made her way past the girl. She was too tired to summon any anger at Felicity's dumb comment. When she reached the door, she paused and addressed her mistress. "I'm sorry I don't meet with your approval," she said in her best company voice. "But you're the one who made me brush your hair twice. If you're late for your guests, it will be your fault, not mine."

Felicity's mouth dropped open. "Why you impertinent little—"

"Excuse me," Andi interrupted, giving the girl a curtsy that would have made her mother proud. "I really must be going."

Before Felicity could recover from her surprise, Andi turned and made a hasty exit, shutting the door quietly behind her.

Chapter Twelve

AN UNPLEASANT EVENING

O nce out of Felicity's sight, a fresh wave of anger revived Andi. She stomped down the stairs. "Patience," she warned herself. "I've got to have money to live on until I find Taffy. I've got to have a job to make some money. Things could be worse." But she didn't know how.

Andi was so busy trying to cool her blazing anger that she didn't notice the huge form of a man coming toward her until she ran into him. She stumbled and fell backward.

The man caught her and balanced her against the wall. "Who are you?" he barked. "Don't you know better than to run into people? Where are your manners?"

Andi stared at the man, speechless. He was the largest person she had ever seen. Much taller than Chad's six feet, this heavyset man towered over her like a giant. His eyebrows formed a thick, black line across his forehead, reminding Andi of an ogre she had once read about in a fairy tale. She swallowed, unable to answer any of his questions.

"She's my new maid, Papa," Felicity said from the top of the stairs. She glided down the staircase and came to stand next to her father.

Mr. Livingston's voice and expression softened at the sight of his daughter. "Well, she sure is clumsy. Let's hope she's an improvement over the last girl. Where did you find her?"

"I don't know. Agatha hired her whole family. Just some Mexican peasants."

"She doesn't look very Mexican to me," Mr. Livingston observed. "I don't know any with blue eyes and freckles on their noses." He grinned and gave Andi a gentle pinch on her cheek. "Does she speak any English?"

"Why don't you ask *me*?" Andi piped up, finding her tongue at last. She rubbed her cheek and scowled at Felicity's father. They were talking about her as if she wasn't even in the room.

Mr. Livingston regarded Andi with amusement. "You have an interesting way about you, for a *Mexican* peasant girl. I'm sure working for Felicity will be an education." He turned to his daughter. "I hope she pleases you, darling."

"She pleases me just fine, Papa." Felicity slipped her hand through her father's arm. "Now, come along. We mustn't keep our guests waiting."

"Andrea!" Mrs. Nelson's call rescued Andi from having to endure more of the conversation. She turned and headed for the kitchen.

When she entered, Mrs. Nelson smiled at her. Her coldness from earlier in the day had disappeared, and she seemed ready to accept Andi as part of her capable staff. "Miss Felicity has kept you busy today, hasn't she?"

"Yes." Andi fell into a nearby chair and let out a weary breath. She glanced at Rosa, who stood at the sink washing pots and pans. Her friend looked tired too. All in all, it had been an exhausting first day on the Lazy L. "May I go now? I'm awfully hungry."

"My goodness, no!" the housekeeper exclaimed. "I need you to help serve the table. You understand and speak English so well. You won't be an embarrassment to the Livingstons in front of their dinner guests. Quite extraordinary, your English." She gave Andi an odd look, then went to the stove and dished some supper into a bowl. "Here. Eat this. It will revive you."

Andi accepted the bowl of food, picked up a spoon, and began to eat. The thick, hot soup was delicious, and Andi felt her spirits rise as her stomach quieted down.

She studied the housekeeper while she ate. Mrs. Nelson's attitude had certainly taken a turn for the better. This morning she had seemed hard and cold. Now she appeared almost friendly.

Mrs. Nelson chatted freely the entire time Andi ate. It didn't take much figuring to discover the reason behind the woman's new attitude. Nila and Rosa had outdone themselves cleaning the house, thus lightening Mrs. Nelson's load considerably.

"And thanks to you, Andrea," she finished, "I was freed from having to tend to Miss Felicity's room and her many demands."

"How old is Felicity?" Andi asked between bites.

"*Miss* Felicity," the housekeeper reminded Andi with a frown. Then she smiled. "She turned sixteen last month. I have known her for many years, since before her dear mother passed away. She is high-spirited, wouldn't you agree?"

Andi shook her head. "No, I don't agree." She took another spoonful of supper. "She's not high-spirited. She's mean and bossy and makes fun of people. Worse, she whips her horse. It's a rotten thing to do!"

Mrs. Nelson caught her breath. "Shame on you, child. It is not your place to criticize your betters." She wiped her hands on her apron and gave Andi her full attention. "You must learn to hold your tongue if you want to continue working here. Felicity does not tolerate disrespect from anyone, especially not from a hired girl. You would do well to remember that."

Andi bowed her head. "I'm sorry. I'm just worn out."

"I'm sure you are," Mrs. Nelson agreed. She checked Andi's bowl. "You're finished? You got enough to eat?"

"Yes, ma'am. It was very good. I feel much better."

"Thank you. I do all the cooking myself. Mr. Livingston trusts no one else in his kitchen." She smiled proudly.

"*Señora,*" Rosa's quiet voice piped up. "I am finished with the pots. What now?"

"Nothing more. You may go," Mrs. Nelson said in her fractured Spanish.

Rosa turned to Andi. "Are you coming?"

"No. I've got to serve supper to the *gringos*."

Rosa gave her a sympathetic look and then escaped out the back door.

The melodic tinkling of a bell sounded from the dining room. Mrs. Nelson hurried toward the stove. She thrust something white toward Andi. "Quickly, Andrea. Put on this apron over your clothes. You must serve the soup."

"Yes, ma'am."

"And for heaven's sake, do not say or do anything unseemly while you are serving. A servant is to be seen and not heard. Do you understand?"

"Yes, ma'am."

Andi picked up the heavy tray and entered the dining room. She immediately felt disoriented. She might know how to set a formal table, but she had no idea how to serve one. At home Luisa set the platters of food on the table, and her family passed them around.

Afraid that at any moment she might drop the heavily laden serving tray, Andi crossed to the sideboard and set the tray down.

"Well? What are you waiting for, Christmas?"

The booming voice from the head of the table startled Andi into action. She began to place the steaming bowls of soup in front of the dinner guests and hoped she was doing it right.

Mr. Livingston sighed and smiled his apologies. "Mrs. Nelson has her hands full training these ignorant Mexicans to do a proper job."

"Indeed," an overdressed, middle-aged woman wheezed. "It's so difficult to get any work out of these lazy foreigners. And they're thieves." She raised a napkin and dabbed her lips. "Randall, didn't you dismiss your last servant for stealing?" Without waiting for a reply, she went on to slander the last maid, her family, and all Mexicans in general.

Andi listened in horror. Did the woman think she couldn't understand her? Felicity certainly knew, yet she did nothing to stop the woman's cruel talk. Never had Andi heard such shameful words about other people.

"I think this girl is doing a fine job," a voice from the opposite end of the table spoke up. He nodded his thanks for the soup. *"Gracias."*

Up until this moment, Andi had avoided eye contact with any of the Livingston dinner guests. She wanted to serve their supper and get out as quickly as her tired arms and legs would let her.

Now Andi looked closer to see which of Mr. Livingston's guests had shown this shred of courtesy. A twinkling brown gaze met hers. She froze. Her heart skipped a beat. Senator James Farley was smiling at her. Did he recognize her, or was his smile simply for the tired-looking, young Mexican girl forced to serve a table full of arrogant *gringos*?

Andi considered. She was dressed in peasant clothes and an apron instead of a fancy dinner dress, with her hair braided rather than brushed out and tied with a bow. She hoped the senator would never consider that Andrea Carter, daughter of one of the wealthiest ranching families in the state, would be serving at a table miles away from home.

I can't let him recognize me, Andi thought. *I'm not ready to go home. I haven't found Taffy yet.*

The senator must have noticed her dismay, for his smile turned to a look of concern. "Are you feeling ill?" he asked in Spanish.

Andi shook her head and placed a bowl of soup in front of Felicity.

Felicity giggled at the senator's comment. "My new servant girl is such a quaint little thing, Senator. She speaks English almost as well as we do. It's so funny to hear her talk."

The senator clearly did not share Felicity's amusement. "Indeed?"

"Yes. It's quite amazing." Felicity smiled. "I believe she's been practicing. Papa says she doesn't look Mexican. Perhaps she's hoping someday to pass for one of us. Isn't that the most amusing thing you ever heard?"

The middle-aged woman broke in with a titter. "The very idea!"

Senator Farley frowned. Apparently he was just as disgusted with the table conversation as she was.

"I'll prove it, Mrs. Thompson," Felicity said.

"I'd prefer you didn't," the senator put in.

Felicity ignored him. "Girl, say something in English for our guests."

Andi gaped at Felicity. Her thoughts spun around like a top. Senator Farley didn't recognize her because he didn't expect to see her here. But as soon as she opened her mouth he'd figure out she was no Mexican servant girl—no matter how hard she tried to act like one. *Besides, I won't let Felicity treat me like a trained parrot.*

She made a snap decision and gave Felicity a blank look. *"Perdón, señorita. ¿Qué decía usted?"*

Senator Farley hid a smile behind his napkin.

Felicity's face turned bright red—clearly a mixture of anger and embarrassment. Her father's face was only one shade lighter.

"Speak in English!" Felicity demanded.

Andi refused to back down. *"¿Cómo?"* She wrinkled her forehead in confusion. *"Lo siento, señorita, pero no entiendo."*

Felicity's father brought his fist down on the table with a force that rattled the dishes. "You understand very well what Miss Felicity said," he said in English. "And as long as you work for me, you will do what you're told, when you're told. Do I make myself clear?"

A dreadful silence fell over the room.

Andi's heart hammered against the inside of her chest. Perhaps she could stand up to Felicity, but she was no match for the furious-looking man glaring at her. She nodded.

"Good. Now bring us the rest of our meal. You can demonstrate your English skills some other time."

Andi fled to the kitchen. She slammed her fists down against the table in much the same way her employer had done.

Mrs. Nelson looked up in surprise. "Good gracious! Whatever is the matter?"

"I won't let Felicity treat me like this!" She went on to describe what had happened.

Mrs. Nelson groaned and wiped her hands on her apron. "Andrea, I warned you. You should have done what she asked. Would it have been so difficult to speak a few words in English? Instead, you embarrassed her in front of her guests." The housekeeper shook her head. "Take care not to defy Miss Felicity again. The horses are not the only ones to feel the brunt of her anger."

Andi laughed at the idea. "She can't hurt me."

"You're on the Lazy L now," Mrs. Nelson said softly, dishing up platters of wonderful-smelling food. "Miss Felicity can do whatever she pleases. The last maid was a girl not much older than you. She stole a handkerchief—or so Miss Felicity says. For that she was dismissed." Mrs. Nelson turned to Andi. Her eyes looked troubled. "She left with a stinging reminder of Miss Felicity's displeasure."

Andi considered this and quickly grew angry. "There was no call for that. Why didn't Mr. Livingston stop her?"

"It is not for you to judge your elders, child. I am simply warning you to be careful."

"If she comes after me with that nasty whip of hers, she'll wish she hadn't," Andi sputtered. "My brothers will teach her some manners in a hurry." She broke off at the look on the housekeeper's face.

"Your *brothers*, child?" Mrs. Nelson cocked her head to one side. "I thought as much. It has not taken me long to notice that although you speak Spanish and dress like the Garduño family, you are not one of them."

"But—"

"You are no more Mexican than I am." Mrs. Nelson smiled, obviously pleased with her deduction. "Your English is flawless, unaccented. I've been watching you ever since you set the table. You do not have the manner of a servant."

Andi felt her cheeks flame.

The housekeeper sighed. "I don't know who you are or why you are with the Mexican family. I suppose that is your own affair. But listen carefully to me. You carry yourself with the confidence and air of a fine family, and that will get you into trouble in this house. It would be better for everyone if you went back to where you came from . . . and soon."

Mrs. Nelson thrust a basket of hot rolls into Andi's hands, effectively cutting off any more discussion. She lifted a heaping platter of fried chicken and nodded toward the door. "Quickly now. We must serve the main course."

Andi reentered the dining room in time to hear Felicity complaining about a horse. She barely listened while she watched Mrs. Nelson place the plate of chicken on the table and return to the kitchen. Andi followed suit, hoping she too could disappear quickly from sight.

"Girl." Randall Livingston's voice stopped Andi in her tracks. "We need our water glasses filled." He nodded toward the pitcher, which sat less than six inches from his empty glass.

Without a word, Andi lifted the heavy pitcher. She made her way around the table, filling glasses and wishing she could give in to the temptation to "accidentally" spill the pitcher's entire contents into Felicity's lap. She was smiling at the thought when she reached for Senator Farley's glass.

The senator caught Andi's gaze and held it. A puzzled expression crossed his face. He opened his mouth to say something, then closed it and shook his head. Instead, he took his glass and whispered, *"Gracias."*

Andi ducked her head and moved on.

"I've had it up to here with that new horse," Felicity was grumbling. "I've tried everything I know to make her mind, but nothing's working."

Her father smiled. "Have you tried making friends with the animal, darling? That has sometimes been known to make a difference."

Felicity pouted. "I tried that already. The mare bit me."

Good for the mare, Andi declared silently, filling another glass with water.

"Have you ridden the horse much?" the young man at Felicity's right asked.

"Ha!" Felicity burst out. "If you can call it that. She lets me mount up. After that, I never know what to expect."

Mr. Livingston put his fork down and gave his daughter a look of surprise. "You've had her for nearly two weeks, Felicity. You should have made progress by this time. Perhaps she's not the right horse for you."

"Oh, but she is, Papa! I know she's the one. She has everything I've been looking for in a horse—beauty, strength, spirit." She narrowed her eyes. "Matt says if I just keep up the training, she'll eventually come around."

"Training?" Mr. Livingston snorted. "You mean whipping, don't you?"

Felicity flushed but said nothing.

Mr. Livingston pointed a finger at her. "Remember what I told you, Felicity. You go easy on this horse, no matter what Matt says. You've already ruined two perfectly good horses because of your impatience. There are other ways—"

"But, Papa," Felicity interrupted. "I want fast results. I want to ride my horse and show her off in front of my friends in town. I won't be thrown again. I won't!"

Her father shrugged and returned to his meal. "I mean what I say, Felicity. I don't want you to come crying to me for a new horse in another month. This is your last chance."

"Oh, Papa, how you do run on! You don't mean that."

The conversation between Felicity and her father continued, but Andi stopped listening. She gripped the water pitcher to keep her hands from shaking. Her heart squeezed in compassion for the poor horse forced to endure Felicity's cruelty. No horse back home had ever felt the sting of the lash. Any wrangler foolish enough to mistreat a horse on the Circle C ranch soon found himself out of a job.

I can't bear this, she thought. *I have to find a way to help that horse.*

"Girl!" Felicity's father shook Andi from her daydreaming. "What's the matter with you? Don't stand there like a simpleton. Finish pouring our water and get back to the kitchen."

Andi finished her task and fled. Mercifully, Mrs. Nelson dismissed her for the evening. Legs quivering with weariness, she stumbled to the small shack she shared with the Garduño family. Although her body was tired, her mind swarmed with plans to rescue Felicity's horse.

Andi sighed. She would no doubt get herself into a heap of trouble, but she couldn't stand by and let Felicity abuse any animal on a whim.

She just couldn't.

Chapter Thirteen

A STARTLING DISCOVERY

The next few days passed in a blur. Felicity kept Andi so busy that she couldn't do anything about the unlucky horse in the barn. Neither did she have a free moment to slip away and question the Lazy L ranch hands about Taffy. When she wasn't dusting or sweeping floors, she was emptying chamber pots, polishing Felicity's boots, or fetching a cool glass of lemonade or a shawl for her mistress.

Felicity delighted in assigning Andi numerous menial tasks to remind her she was nothing more than a servant. Worse, the older girl never seemed satisfied with Andi's work. A harsh tongue-lashing greeted her every morning. Andi had never been bossed around so much in her whole life. Felicity's demands made Chad's bossing look like gentle requests by comparison.

I never thought I would miss Chad's yelling, but I do. She smiled grimly. *At least I can holler back at him.*

Late one morning, Andi lifted the heavy bucket of water she'd used when Mrs. Nelson ordered her to scrub the kitchen floor and hauled it out the back door. The scent of lilacs and roses greeted her.

She took a deep breath and sighed. Andi almost wished Senator Farley had recognized her at supper the other night. He'd have seen her safely home by now, and perhaps it would have been for the best.

Her stay on the Lazy L certainly hadn't brought Andi any closer to finding Taffy, nor did it seem likely she'd have time this morning to wander around the ranch and question the cowhands. Mrs. Nelson had gone into town with a long list of errands and left Andi, Rosa, and Nila with the unhappy chore of scouring the kitchen from floor to ceiling. It would probably take the rest of the day. Nila had been busy since sunrise cleaning out ashes and blacking the huge cookstove.

Andi tossed the dirty water from the bucket onto the flower bed that bordered the kitchen porch. She dropped the bucket to the ground and leaned against a post, enjoying the sun on her face. She closed her eyes and let the warmth creep into her tired body.

She was just deciding she could rest a few minutes longer when she heard a tremendous crash. Her eyes flew open. From the barn came more crashing, the high-pitched whinny of a horse in pain, and a loud shrieking.

Rosa came running onto the back porch. "What is that noise?" she whispered in a frightened voice.

Andi shook her head. "Something's going on in the barn. I don't know what." She took a step off the porch. Her heart pounded at the terror in the horse's cry.

The shrieks became angry words. "Stupid, unmanageable horse!"

Andi recognized the voice, and it turned her blood to ice. Even from this distance, she could hear the slap of Felicity's riding crop. She clenched her fists when the horse screamed again. Her decision to rescue the animal came back in full force and swept all weariness away.

"Oh, Rosa!" Andi clutched her friend's arm for support. "Felicity is at it again. I can't stand it. I've got to do something."

"No, mi amiga." Rosa shook her head. "Come away. Forget the horse." She pulled Andi back on the porch. "The *señorita* terrifies me. You must not cross her."

"I have to rescue that horse," Andi said. "I'll ride her home and ask for help finding Taffy—like I should have done days ago." She set her jaw and jerked her chin toward the barn. "Taffy can wait, but the poor horse in there can't."

Her decision made, Andi snatched up the bucket and hurried into the kitchen. Rosa scurried after her, shaking her head and mumbling her disapproval of Andi's plan.

"I need more rags," Nila said, turning from the stove. "They are in the bin across from—" She frowned. "What has happened?"

Andi dropped the bucket on the floor and took a deep breath. "It's time for me to go home, *señora*."

Nila's face broke into a wide smile. She nodded her agreement. "You have come to your senses at last." She turned to her daughter. "Is this not wonderful news, Rosita?"

Rosa appeared too upset to reply.

Andi crossed over to Nila and lowered her voice. "I'm going to do a very bad thing, *señora*. I'm going to steal a horse." Before Nila could express her astonishment, Andi went on. "I don't want to, but I've got to get the horse away from Felicity, at least for a little while."

"Don't let her do it, *Mamá*," Rosa pleaded, wringing her hands.

Nila trembled and shook her head. "This is a foolish and dangerous idea, Andrea. If you are caught, you will be punished. The law will not care that you are only a child."

Nila was right. Andi's only hope lay in getting the abused horse back to the Circle C before any sheriff caught up with her. Once home, she would be safe. Her family would protect her, no matter how foolish she had been.

"I know." She nodded. "I'm not going to do it in broad daylight. I'll sneak away tonight when everyone's asleep."

Nila sighed her acceptance and drew Andi into a warm hug. "Well then, *chiquita, vaya con Dios*. May He guide you safely home."

"Go with God," Rosa echoed, sniffing back tears. She threw her arms around Andi. "I will miss you."

"I'll miss you too." Andi drew away from her friends and forced a smile. "I'll be right back to help you. But first I want to see which stall the horse is in so I can find it after dark."

Andi stepped onto the porch and nearly collided with the housekeeper, who was striding purposefully toward the door. "Mrs. Nelson," she stammered, skipping out of the woman's path. "You're back so soon. Did you forget something?"

"I wish to speak with you, Andrea," Mrs. Nelson said. Her eyes blazed. "Immediately."

Andi swallowed her surprise and followed the unsmiling woman into the house. At Rosa's questioning look, Andi shrugged. She had no idea why the housekeeper wanted to see her.

Mrs. Nelson marched through the kitchen, pausing only long enough to remove her hat and shawl before continuing her brisk walk down the hallway. Her heels clicked noisily against the wooden floor. When she reached the library, she stopped and motioned Andi to enter. Then she followed behind and slid the doors shut with a resounding *clunk*.

Silence fell. Andi watched uneasily while Mrs. Nelson unfolded a piece of paper she was clutching in her hand. It grew in size until Andi recognized a Wanted poster similar to others she'd seen hanging in the sheriff's office in Fresno.

Mrs. Nelson thrust the paper toward Andi. "I came across this in town. It might interest you."

Andi took the poster from Mrs. Nelson with a trembling hand. She stared in dismay at the letters screaming at her from across the top of the page: **MISSING!** And under it, more bold lettering: **REWARD: $1,000**. A fair likeness of herself mocked her from below the words. Her eyes blurred when she read her name.

"Oh, no," she murmured in a choked voice.

"You're Elizabeth Carter's girl," Mrs. Nelson stated bluntly.

Andi nodded, speechless.

The housekeeper snatched the poster from Andi's hand and refolded it. Then she stuffed it into her sleeve. "This is a fine kettle of fish," she scolded. "The Carters are an important family in this part of California. A respected family. You should not be working as a servant to the Livingstons. It's shameful. As of right now, you are dismissed. Pack your things. Someone will take you to the railroad depot. You're going home."

"But—"

"Do as I say at once," Mrs. Nelson insisted. "The train leaves in an hour."

Andi bit back her protest and followed the housekeeper out of the library and down the hall. Through eyes blurred with unshed tears, she left the house and started toward the small cabin she shared with the Garduño family. She would change into her overalls and return the skirt and blouse Nila had lent her.

Now I won't get a chance to free the horse, she moaned silently. *What will happen to it?*

Andi threw a final, sorrowful glance toward the barn and paused in surprise. Felicity was standing in the corral, waving her hands and shouting at a dusty cowhand. Behind her, an obviously upset horse tossed its head and whinnied. The cowhand held tightly to the horse's bridle.

"Well?" Felicity demanded. "Can I ride her or not?"

The young man gave the bridle a vicious jerk and whacked the trembling animal. "Why sure, Miss Felicity. I reckon you can do anything you set your mind to. Just give it another try."

Felicity positioned one foot in the stirrup and glared at the ranch hand. "Don't you dare let go," she ordered, tucking her riding crop under her arm. She reached up and caught the saddle horn. Then she hoisted herself carefully onto the horse's back. "So far, so good." She nodded at the cowhand. He released the bridle and left the corral to join a group of interested onlookers lounging against the barn.

Fascinated with the scene, Andi rubbed her eyes and hurried over to the corral. She climbed onto the lowest railing and leaned over the top of the fence. Then she took a good, long look at Felicity's horse.

Andi reeled. She let go of the railing and staggered backward, shaking her head in disbelief. *Taffy?*

It can't be! she silently screamed. It would be better if Taffy were lost forever than to be here, mistreated and frightened. *It's another palomino*, Andi reasoned. *It has to be.*

Sick to her stomach, but realizing she had to discover the truth, Andi crept back to the fence. She peered between the railings at the horse and rider.

Felicity trotted around the corral, waving her whip and laughing shrilly. "I knew I could break her," she shouted. "The mare just needed to learn who's boss. Look at me, Matt! I—"

The palomino stopped short. Felicity flew over her head and landed on the ground like a sack of feed. She groaned.

Andi clapped a hand over her mouth to smother her astonishment. Her gaze swept over the horse. Her heart squeezed. It *was* Taffy. Her four white socks, the white blaze on her nose, the creamy mane and tail. Andi didn't need to see the brand mark to know she'd found her horse.

She watched Taffy trot away from the moaning figure lying in the dust. "Good for you, Taffy," she whispered.

Felicity rose shakily to her feet. She hurried after Taffy and snatched up the reins. With her free hand, she brought the riding crop down across the mare's neck. "I'll teach you not to throw me."

Taffy shuddered and tossed her head, snorting her fear and anger. She tried to shy away from the stinging blows, but Felicity held her fast.

With a cry of outrage, Andi threw open the corral gate. She raced across the enclosure and planted herself between Felicity and Taffy. "Don't you *dare* hit this horse!" Andi clenched her fists to keep from striking the girl.

Felicity's face showed her surprise. "What business is it of yours? She's my horse. I'll do as I please with her. As for you . . ." Her eyes narrowed. "What are you doing out here? Get back to work."

Andi ignored her. She reached out and threw her arms around Taffy's neck, burying her face in the mare's creamy mane. Taffy immediately settled down. She nuzzled Andi's neck and nickered softly.

"Oh, Taffy," Andi murmured in the mare's ear. "I found you at last."

A crack like a bee sting caught Andi across her shoulders. She yelped and whirled.

"Get your filthy hands off my horse," Felicity ordered between clenched teeth. She raised her whip to emphasize her command.

Burning anger exploded inside Andi. This time she didn't try to control it. She flew at Felicity and yanked the whip from her hand. Clutching the riding crop, she looked at her golden horse. Thin, red cuts crisscrossed Taffy's neck and flank.

"I'd like to give you a good dose of what you gave my horse." Andi raised the riding crop but couldn't bring herself to hit Felicity. Her initial fury began to wane. No matter how much Andi wanted to beat the girl, she would not do it. She flung the whip away in disgust.

"*Your* horse?" A dark flush crept up Felicity's neck and into her cheeks. "How dare you? Get away from here, you impudent girl."

Andi reached out and caught hold of Taffy's bridle. "Don't worry. We're leaving." She stroked Taffy's nose and whispered, "It's all over now. I won't let her hurt you again."

"The horse stays," Felicity said. "My father bought her. If you take her, you'll be stealing." She drew a deep, shaky breath. "I'm warning you . . ."

Andi turned her back on Felicity and mounted Taffy in one smooth motion. Sitting astride her horse, she felt at peace for the first time since leaving home. She was glad she didn't have to steal an unknown horse to save it from Felicity's abuse. Taking back her own mare didn't bother Andi's conscience one bit. She felt only a weary sense of relief that she could return to her family at last, ask forgiveness, and accept the punishment she knew she deserved.

104

"Come on, Taffy," she said. "Let's get out of here."

Taffy leaped into a lope, clearly as anxious as Andi to be free of the Lazy L. They flew through the open gate of the corral and down the broad lane leading to the road.

"Come back here!" Felicity shrieked.

Andi glanced over her shoulder to see Felicity running here and there, ordering the men to give chase. Three of the hired hands mounted up and galloped after her.

Andi grinned. Taffy could easily outrun those cow ponies. The thrill of a race surged through her. "Go, Taffy!"

Taffy broke into a gallop.

Less than a minute later, Andi's joy turned to dismay. A group of men were riding up the driveway toward her. She groaned. *They must be more Lazy L hands.*

"Stop her!" Felicity's voice was faint but clear. "She's stealing my horse!"

The men went into action. They spread themselves out across the wide lane, blocking Taffy's forward movement.

Trapped on either side by hundreds of yards of white fencing, Andi realized she had little choice but to stop. To jump the fence on such short notice was too risky. She slowed Taffy to a walk and allowed the hands to escort her back to the ranch.

When Andi returned to the corral, Felicity was waiting for her. Her eyes glinted dangerously. Her lips twisted into a sneer. Without a word, she seized Taffy's bridle and yanked the horse to an abrupt halt.

Andi swallowed in sudden fear. Maybe—just maybe—she should have hazarded the jump, after all.

Chapter Fourteen

TRAPPED!

Get off my horse and off my father's ranch, you thief!" Felicity grasped Andi's arm. "I never want to see you again." She dragged Andi from the saddle and gave her a rough shove, which sent her tumbling to the ground.

It was a bad mistake. Taffy snorted, sidestepped, then stretched out her neck and nipped Felicity on the arm.

Felicity yelped and jumped back, rubbing her arm. "The mare bit me! She drew blood." Her eyes widened in shock and pain. "She'll pay for that." Felicity glanced around the corral. "I'll teach this horse a lesson she won't ever forget."

Andi spotted the discarded whip at the same instant Felicity did. With her heart in her throat, Andi scooped it up and sprinted away. Fear for Taffy replaced her anger at Felicity. She glanced wildly around the yard, searching for an adult—*any* adult—who would keep Felicity from carrying out her plans. Her gaze fell on a small group of ranch hands near the barn.

"Oh, please!" she shouted, throwing herself to the top of the corral railing. "You've got to stop her. Taffy's too good a horse to be whipped. Felicity will ruin her."

One of the ranch hands shook his head. It was obvious he wanted no part of this scuffle. He walked away and disappeared behind the barn.

A young hand scratched his chin. "Maybe we oughta—"

"Don't be a fool," an old-timer warned. He snagged the man's shirt sleeve and pulled him along.

"You miserable cowards!" Andi yelled.

"Nah, they ain't cowards," the remaining cowhand remarked. "They just know the only orders that count on this ranch come from the boss or Miss Felicity." He pushed back his hat and shrugged. "It's her horse. Besides, a lick or two never hurt no horse—especially a stubborn one."

The cowhand folded his arms across his chest and spat a stream of tobacco juice in Andi's direction. Then he sauntered off toward the bunkhouse.

Andi dropped from the railing, turned around, and ran smack into Felicity. The older girl ripped the crop from Andi's hand and gave her a shove. "Stay out of my way."

Andi stumbled backward but quickly regained her footing. She clenched her fists and hurried after Felicity. "You're a wicked, wicked girl to whip a good horse just because you can't manage her any other way."

A sudden, painful tightening around her arm told Andi her comment had struck home. "I've taken as much as I'm going to take from the likes of you," Felicity hissed. "And this horse is never going to bite me again."

"You deserve to be bitten," Andi shot back. She wrenched herself free from Felicity's grip and threw her arms around Taffy's neck. "I won't let you touch her."

"We'll see about that." Felicity took a step away from the pair. She shook her head. "You should never have tried to steal my horse."

"I didn't steal your horse," Andi said. "Look at the brand. Circle C. She's a Carter horse, and I'm Andrea Carter."

"Ha. And I'm the governor's daughter," Felicity mocked. "As if I'd believe you. You're nothing but a servant girl and a thief." Felicity raised her whip. "Step aside . . . *or else.*"

Andi clung to Taffy's neck and tried to think. *Or else what?* Felicity couldn't go after Taffy so long as Andi stood between them. But she couldn't stay here forever. Sooner or later Felicity would get Taffy alone.

What can I say to change her mind? "Please, Felicity," she pleaded, her throat so tight she could hardly speak. "Don't hit her. I'll show you how to handle her. I'll help you—"

"*You!* Help *me?*" Felicity's laugh was a loud bark. "Never. This horse will learn things *my* way. Now, get away from my horse."

Andi gulped back her fear and stood her ground. "No, Felicity. You won't whip Taffy. Not if I can help it."

Felicity sprang forward. She yanked Andi away from Taffy and slammed her to the ground.

Andi lay still and tried to catch her breath. She shook her head to clear it. Any moment, she expected to hear the whistling of the whip and her horse's terrified whinnies. When nothing happened, she looked up. Felicity towered over her, the riding crop poised to strike.

"Felicity, no!" Andi shouted in sudden, awful understanding. Had Felicity lost her mind? Andi scrambled to her feet.

The first stroke of Felicity's riding whip across her back sent Andi to the ground gasping. A wave of pain and humiliation washed over her. She heard Felicity's triumphant chuckle and tried to rise. But before Andi could scurry away, the second blow fell. She clenched her jaw to keep from crying out.

"This will put you in your place, thief," Felicity murmured, striking her a third time, then fourth. "Then I'll deal with my horse."

"She's . . . not . . . your . . . horse." Andi forced the words out between breaths. She threw herself beneath Taffy's belly in an attempt to avoid Felicity's quick, stinging blows. She crawled to the other side of her horse and stood up, clutching Taffy's creamy mane for support.

Tears flooded Andi's eyes, but she blinked them back. *She can't make me cry!* She took a deep, shuddering breath.

Felicity appeared at Taffy's rear. She raised her crop and brought it down with a loud *whack* against the mare's rump. Taffy screamed and bolted, sending Andi to the ground in a crumpled heap.

"Felicity!" Mr. Livingston's voice sliced the air like a knife.

Andi looked up. Felicity's father was approaching the corral in long, angry strides. An obviously distraught Mrs. Nelson followed at his heels. With a mighty shove, the big man threw open the gate and stalked over to his daughter.

"Have you taken leave of your senses?" Mr. Livingston tore the whip from Felicity's hand. He glanced down at Andi with a worried frown. "Are you all right, girl?"

"I feel sick." Andi swallowed hard and made no move to get up. Instead, she tried to keep her roiling stomach from disgracing her. Any second, her breakfast would come up. She closed her eyes to shut out the pain. *I want my mother.* Her eyes stung with unshed tears.

"See to the girl," Mr. Livingston instructed Mrs. Nelson. Then he turned back to Felicity. "I thought I made it clear this sort of thing was not to happen again."

"It was an accident, Papa," Felicity explained in a small voice. "The horse bit me." She thrust out her arm. "Look." Dried blood covered a bite the size of a half dollar. "I was disciplining the mare, and the girl got in the way."

Mr. Livingston pierced his daughter with a dark gaze. "She got in the way? That's it? Nothing more?"

Felicity shrugged. "All right. She stole my horse. Just mounted the mare and galloped off. When I confronted her, she attacked me."

Andi gulped back the bile that rose to her throat. "All I did was take away her whi—"

"I couldn't let her steal my horse, could I?" Felicity cut in with a pout.

Mr. Livingston whirled on Andi, clearly bewildered at this new information. "Why would you steal Felicity's horse?"

"She's n-not Felicity's horse," Andi stammered. "She's mine."

"That's ridiculous," Felicity stormed. "An outright lie."

Mrs. Nelson glanced up from Andi's side. "Sir, this child needs tending. It looks like she took a pretty good whipping before you got here."

Mr. Livingston waved his housekeeper's concern away. "She looks all right to me, Agatha. Just send her back to her cabin for the rest of the day. She'll be fine by tomorrow morning."

Mrs. Nelson helped Andi to her feet and fixed an unyielding gaze on her employer. "You asked me to see to this girl. She is *not* all right. It would be much wiser to settle her in the guest room and ask Dr. Tanner to take a look at her injuries."

"The guest room?" Mr. Livingston's brows shot up. "Why in the world . . ."

His voice trailed off when Mrs. Nelson reached into her sleeve and withdrew the notice Andi had seen only a short time ago. "You had better take a look at this before you decide anything."

Mr. Livingston took the paper from her hand. "What's this all about?"

"Read it," Mrs. Nelson said.

Silence fell over the corral while Felicity's father scanned the page. When he finished he let out a long, deep sigh and looked at Andi. "I don't think Doc Tanner's services are required." He returned his gaze to the poster. "The fewer people who know about this, the better."

He glanced at Felicity, who stood quietly a few feet away, shoulders slumped. Her eyes no longer held the wild, angry look Andi had seen earlier. "I have my daughter's reputation to consider. Her emotions are fragile. I won't have her upset."

Mrs. Nelson drew herself up to her full height and faced the huge man. "It's not a peasant child stealing a handkerchief *this* time," she reminded him. "You won't be able to cover it up so easily. When Elizabeth Carter learns what Felicity did to her daughter—"

"That will be enough, Agatha," Mr. Livingston snapped. "You forget yourself. I can handle the Carters."

Mrs. Nelson clamped her jaw shut, but her eyes smoldered with disapproval.

"Do what you think best for the girl's injuries," Mr. Livingston said, "but leave that money-grubbing Doc Tanner out of this." He tapped his finger on the poster. "He'd wire Fresno quicker than you can say 'reward.'"

Mr. Livingston crumpled the poster into a ball and crammed it into his pocket. Then he turned and stalked out of the corral.

Andi sat on the window seat of the Livingstons' elegant guest room and gazed through the glass. She could see her beautiful, golden palomino standing patiently in the corral. Taffy shook her head, and her creamy mane flew in all directions. She flicked her ears forward in an attitude of anticipation, as if she expected her true mistress to return at any moment.

Two ranch hands entered the corral and led the mare toward the barn. Taffy did not go willingly. She reared and flailed her legs in protest.

Andi clenched her fists at the sight, helpless to do anything about it. She turned from the window in despair. A lump grew in her throat until she couldn't swallow. She blinked furiously to keep her tears in check.

"Andrea?" Nila's kind voice echoed softly in the room.

Andi looked up. Her Mexican friend carried a basin and towel, which she set on a small table. She crossed to the window seat and sat down. Placing one of Andi's small hands in her own, she gave it a gentle squeeze. "I am so sorry, *chiquita*. I wish we had never come to this *rancho*."

Andi drew a shaky breath and shook her head. "Don't say that.

After all, I found my horse." She glanced back toward the window, but Taffy had disappeared.

"True. But at what price?"

Andi bowed her head. "It hurts, *señora*. It feels like a thousand bees are stinging my back. I want my mother."

"Of course you do." Nila pulled her into a gentle embrace, mindful of Andi's injured back. "Now, come lie down on the bed while I tend your wounds."

Andi made her way over to the huge, four-poster bed and climbed up. She sprawled out on her stomach and buried her head in the feather pillow. Then she squeezed her eyes shut and waited.

Nila gently lifted the back of Andi's blouse. "This may sting a little," she warned, reaching for the basin. With gentle hands, she began to gently probe and clean the worst of the welts.

"Are you almost finished?" Andi asked a few minutes later. She dug her fingers into the pillow to keep from crying out.

"*Sí,*" Nila replied. "I am applying the salve now."

Andi shuddered when the cold mixture touched her bare skin. Then she felt her blouse being lowered. She sat up. "*Gracias, señora.*"

Nila nodded and began to gather up the towels and medicine.

Suddenly, without any warning or the courtesy of a knock, the door flew open. Randall Livingston entered the room. "So, how's the patient?" he asked cheerfully.

Andi scowled at the intruder. "It's not polite to enter a room without knocking."

Mr. Livingston chuckled and settled himself at the foot of the bed. "You're certainly full of sass today. That's good. It means you're not seriously hurt, except maybe for your stubborn Carter pride."

Andi looked at him blankly.

Mr. Livingston crossed his arms and leaned against the bedpost. "I know your family, Miss Carter. Who doesn't? I've had dealings with them. Chad Carter doesn't like to lose." He smiled. "And apparently neither do you."

Andi wrinkled her forehead. "What are you talking about?"

"Felicity told me the whole story," he replied. "This scuffle between you girls was nothing more than a misunderstanding. You lost but refuse to accept it."

"That's not true!"

"You made a mistake. Felicity reacted poorly. She should not have hit you, of course, but you did provoke her." He shrugged. "A few days of rest—maybe a week or two—and you'll agree this incident was just a silly quarrel not worth remembering."

"A week or two?" Andi gaped at the man in disbelief. "I'm going home *today*. Mrs. Nelson said so. Now that I've found my horse I—"

"I'm afraid not, Miss Carter," Mr. Livingston cut in. "I can't allow you to return to your family in your present condition. Your mother might read more into this incident than I'd like. She could make my life difficult. For Felicity's sake, you will stay here until you are completely healed from your . . . *accident*. Then it will be only your word against mine."

"What about my horse?"

"That's between you and Felicity. However"—Mr. Livingston caught Andi's gaze and held it—"I recommend you give up the horse, for your own sake." He stood up and crossed the room. When he reached the door, he paused. "One more thing, Miss Carter. Consider yourself my guest for the next several days. This is your room. Please don't leave it. As long as you honor my request and behave like a guest, I will treat you as one. Do anything that brings shame to Felicity, and you will pay the price."

Andi gulped back her dismay at the man's words. She was trapped, but good.

Chapter Fifteen

FELICITY'S PLAN

As soon as the guest room door clicked shut, Andi burst into tears. She'd held them back all during her encounter with Felicity and refused to cry even one drop. Soon she'd be home, and all this would be a passing nightmare.

Wrong.

Two more weeks? Andi buried her head in the pillow and sobbed her heart out. She couldn't bear to be away from her family for two more weeks, especially now. She'd found Taffy, but her mare was in danger while she was anywhere near Felicity.

Nila grasped Andi by the shoulders and began hushing her in quiet tones. Andi relaxed and rolled over to face her friend, wincing when her blouse rubbed against her sore back.

"The *señor* said something that upset you," Nila said.

Andi nodded and sat up. "He won't let me go home. He says it's nothing more than a silly argument and wants to keep Felicity from taking any blame for what she did to me. He can't see how cruel and selfish she really is. Worst of all, he won't give me my horse."

Fresh tears threatened to spill. Andi rubbed her eyes. Crying did no good. It didn't even make her feel better—only worse.

Nila clucked in sympathy. "I am so sorry. What a pity!"

Andi bit her lip and tried to think. Would Mr. Livingston keep her locked in this room? Even if he didn't and she somehow managed to sneak out of the house, how would she leave the ranch? Steal another horse?

No, Andi decided. That hadn't worked the first time. There were too many people lingering around the yard to escape unnoticed. She paused. Perhaps there was another way.

"Señora," she said, "I need your help. You've got to send a wire—a telegram—to the Circle C ranch near Fresno. I'll write it out, and José can go to town and send it. My family will come for me. I know they will."

At Andi's words, Nila's face lost all color. She clasped her hands together and shook her head. "Please, *chiquita*. Do not ask this of us."

"Why not?" Andi asked in surprise. "It's easy. Take Rosa. She knows enough English to send a telegram."

"It's not that." Nila rose and began pacing the room. "You don't understand. *Señor* Livingston knows you are not one of us. José is afraid the law will come for him because we kept you with us."

"I'll explain. No one would blame you."

Nila wrung her hands. "Your word will mean nothing if this important *ranchero* decides to cause trouble for us. We have heard tales of such happenings . . ." Her voice trailed off into silence.

Andi gazed into the woman's dark, frightened eyes. "You're really afraid, aren't you?"

Nila nodded. "We are strangers in a country we know nothing about, wanting only to live in peace. You have been much help to us over the past few weeks, and we are grateful. However, I'm afraid José will not agree to send a telegram." Her eyes brimmed with tears. "I am so sorry, *chiquita*."

Andi knew her friend was torn up inside at her decision. *"Está bien, señora,"* she assured her, even though it really wasn't all right at all. "I'll think of something else."

Nila nodded her thanks and scooped up the basin and towels. "I must get back to work," she said. "Perhaps the *señora* will allow me to return later in the day. *Adiós, chiquita.*"

But Nila did not come back.

Mrs. Nelson, looking grimmer than ever, brought Andi her supper tray and news of the Garduño family. "They're gone," she explained in answer to Andi's question. "Mr. Livingston dismissed them, along with a few parting words of advice."

What the advice was, Mrs. Nelson would not say, but Andi could guess. It chilled her to the bone. She opened her mouth to plead with the housekeeper to help her, but a new voice broke in.

"Good heavens, Agatha," Felicity exclaimed, hurrying into the guest room. She clutched a small lap desk tightly against her chest. "So now you're bringing this . . . this . . . housemaid a supper tray?" She stood beside the bed, scowling at Mrs. Nelson.

Mrs. Nelson regarded Felicity silently for a moment. Then she spoke. "I have work to do, so if you'll excuse me?" She turned and left.

Felicity ignored the disapproval in the housekeeper's voice. Her gaze darted around the room before coming to rest on Andi. "I see Papa has decided to treat you like a guest rather than the servant you are." She jerked her chin toward the tray. "Your supper's getting cold."

Andi didn't care. She'd lost her appetite the minute Felicity appeared in the doorway.

"Meals in your room. Leisure time." Felicity smirked. "All you lack now are decent clothes to replace those peasant rags you're wearing."

Andi bristled at the mocking tone but held her tongue.

Felicity settled herself into a large, overstuffed chair in the corner of the room. She set her lap desk on her knees, opened it, and took out a piece of paper. When she spoke, the change in her voice put Andi instantly on guard. "I've been thinking all afternoon, Andrea," she said pleasantly. "Perhaps we can avoid another misunderstanding if I draw up an agreement between us."

"What sort of agreement?" Andi asked.

Felicity brought the paper over to the bed and dropped it in Andi's lap. "It's a bill of sale. Quite ordinary."

Andi frowned. "A bill of sale for what?"

"You know perfectly well what it's for," Felicity snapped, eyes blazing. She looked ready to strike. Then she smiled, took a deep breath, and composed herself. "There's going to be trouble over that silly horse. We can't both have her. I admit she may have belonged to you at one time but—"

"Brand marks don't lie," Andi cut in.

"Even if she did belong to you," Felicity went on as if Andi had not interrupted her, "she's mine now. I want you to sign this bill of sale to make it all nice and legal. In return . . ." She fished around in a small purse and brought out two shiny gold coins. "I'm prepared to pay you twenty dollars as a token of my goodwill."

Goodwill? Andi gaped at Felicity. What did this cruel, selfish girl know about goodwill? She'd treated Andi worse than a slave since the day she arrived. She'd abused Andi's precious horse, and then whipped Andi until Mr. Livingston stepped in. Worse, Felicity had twisted her story into a lie to escape blame.

Now she wants me to sign over Taffy for twenty dollars? Andi shook her head. *She's crazy.*

"Well?" Felicity prodded when Andi didn't answer. "What do you say?"

Andi was so astonished at the girl's outrageous attempt to keep Taffy that she didn't know *what* to say. She picked up the paper and scanned it. It looked like a real bill of sale. Just like the ones she'd seen Justin fill out.

There was a detailed description of Taffy, her previous owner, new owner, price paid, date—even her brand mark. Near the bottom of the page a long, black line shouted for a signature.

"Here." Felicity held out an ink-filled pen.

Andi shook her head. "Here's what I think of your offer." She ripped the bill of sale in two. "You're *loco* if you think I'd sell you

117

any horse—much less my best friend." She let the two halves flutter to the floor. "Go away and leave me alone."

Felicity's face turned a dull red. She bent down to pick up the torn bill of sale. "You'll be sorry you did that." She stuffed the papers into her lap desk. "*Very* sorry." She left the room, slamming the door with such force it shook the walls.

Ⓒ

Squeak. The noise jerked Andi from a troubled sleep. She opened her eyes and looked around. It wasn't quite dawn, judging by the amount of light trickling through the lace curtains of the guest room. What had awakened her? She listened. All was still.

Hearing nothing, Andi snuggled deeper under the warm quilts. She wished she could fall asleep and wake up in her own bed. "How many times have I wished *that* these past couple of weeks?" she mumbled bitterly.

She winced as she tried to find a comfortable position. The sharp, stinging pain from yesterday's encounter with Felicity had dulled to a steady ache. As long as she lay still and made no quick movements, it was bearable.

Andi yawned and pulled the quilt closer around her shoulders. *Go to sleep*, she commanded her whirling thoughts. *Don't think about anything but—*

Without warning, an icy hand clamped down over her mouth. Andi screamed, but it came out a muffled yelp. Her heart raced. She struggled to sit up.

"Hush," came a whispered command. "Do you want to wake the entire household?"

Andi stopped struggling. Her pounding heart returned to normal. She reached up and pried Felicity's fingers from her face. "What are you doing here?" she demanded in a harsh whisper.

Felicity released her and stepped back. She lit the lamp on the bedside table. "It's the mare," she explained, adjusting the flame to a dim yellow glow. "I think she's in bad shape. She won't let Matt or me near her, but she might let you approach."

"*Taffy?*" Andi threw off the quilts and leaped from her bed. Her back screamed a protest, but she ignored the pain and raced for the door.

Felicity snatched her arm. "You can't go out in your nightgown. Get dressed. Hurry."

Andi yanked the white cotton nightgown over her head and tossed it to the floor. She shivered in the chilly, predawn air and pulled on the blouse and skirt Nila had given her. Then she slipped on her boots and stumbled for the door.

"Come quietly," Felicity warned her. "Papa's a light sleeper. Remember, you're not supposed to be out of your room."

Andi gave a hurried nod and let Felicity go first. The older girl, dressed in a riding skirt and warm jacket, led Andi down the stairs and through the kitchen. Placing a finger to her lips, she cracked open the back door and motioned Andi out into the cool, fresh new day.

Fear washed over Andi as she sprinted toward the barn. "What are her symptoms? Is it colic? Did she get into the grain?" She forced the questions out between breaths. "Can she stand?"

Felicity shook her head and kept running. She raced ahead of Andi and disappeared into the barn.

When Andi reached the barn's double doors, she was panting from her run and from her fear for Taffy's life. She paused to catch her breath. Her heart pounded. She knew next to nothing about treating sick horses. That was Chad's job, and he did it well. If only he were here now!

If Taffy sickens and dies, it'll be all my fault. Oh, please, God! Don't let her die.

A new thought gave Andi hope. Perhaps Felicity's father was a good stockman. As soon as she checked Taffy, she'd run for Mr. Livingston, even if it meant waking him up and putting up with his wrath.

Felicity's voice called to Andi from the dimly lit barn. "In here!"

Andi hurried inside, calling Taffy's name. She heard an answering whinny and caught a glimpse of a healthy, alert golden palomino before something rough and smelly was thrown over her head.

Then everything went dark.

Chapter Sixteen

GOOD-BYE, TAFFY

It took Andi only a few breaths to realize she'd been tricked. Horribly tricked! She was so angry, frightened, and humiliated that she wanted to scream and kick. She could do neither. Strong arms—obviously not Felicity's—wrapped the burlap sack tightly around Andi's body and lifted her into a wagon.

"Felicity!" she managed to gasp, struggling for air.

There was no answer, only a pair of firm hands keeping her flat against the wagon bed. She tried to wriggle free, but her back exploded in pain from the movement. She bit her lip and lay still.

"Hurry, Matt," Felicity whispered from close by. "Let's get moving."

When the rattling and jostling of the wagon finally ceased, Andi could tell through the rough weave of the burlap that the sky had begun to lighten. She didn't resist when Matt hauled her from the wagon and slung her over his shoulder. A set of keys jangled, a door creaked open, and Andi fell to the ground with a groan. Rough hands yanked at the burlap sack, and in a moment she was free.

With one quick glance, Andi took in her surroundings. She was sitting on a dirt floor in an old, deserted storage shed no larger than her horse's stall back home. It was stoutly built of strong, rough-hewn logs. The only light, a pale slice of the early morning sky, came from about seven feet up through narrow gaps in the roof. A sturdy door with rusting hinges discouraged thieves from breaking in and stealing whatever had once been stored here.

When Andi's eyes adjusted to the dim interior, she could make out a few pieces of broken farm equipment hanging from wooden pegs protruding from the walls. A pile of tattered feed sacks—thoroughly chewed by rodents—lay in a heap in one corner. It was apparent that no one had used this shed for years.

Felicity smiled. "What do you think of my little hideaway? I found it a few years ago, hidden in this little gully away from everything." She shrugged. "The remains of an old cabin are close by. I'd guess it's at least thirty years old. It most likely belonged to some old prospector who never struck it rich and decided to try his hand at farming instead."

"Why, Felicity?" Andi asked, ignoring the history lesson. "Why did you trick me?"

Felicity sighed. "I couldn't very well kidnap you from your room in broad daylight. Too many prying eyes. But I knew exactly how to get you to the barn without a struggle, at a time when no one would be up. Matt was more than willing to help me." She glanced up at the tall, lanky cowboy. "He's sweet on me."

Matt grinned and leaned against the doorjamb, arms crossed.

"I don't understand any of this," Andi said. "Why am I here?"

Felicity shook her head. "I knew you'd never sign the bill of sale as long as you stayed comfortable in my father's guest room." She spread her arms to indicate the shed. "On the other hand, this *new* room will help you decide much more quickly to do as I say. I told you yesterday you'd be sorry. Are you sorry yet?"

Andi felt herself pale. "Not as sorry as *you're* going to be. Your father will hit the ceiling when he finds out I've disappeared."

Felicity snorted. "Oh, Papa will fuss and fume for a few days, but he'll never suspect I had anything to do with it. Why should he? He's more likely to believe you slipped away and headed for home, too frightened and hurting to give any more thought to a horse."

Andi's stomach turned over. Felicity made it sound so reasonable.

"Besides, once the horse is mine, I won't care what Papa thinks. It will all turn out to be nothing more than a tempest in a teapot." Felicity dusted off her skirt and pulled a folded paper from her jacket pocket. "Now, down to business."

Andi sighed wearily. "I'm not signing it. If you try to make me, I'll just tear it up again."

"We'll see," Felicity said. "It's simple. When you sign it, I'll let you leave this shed. Until then"—she glanced around—"consider yourself at home."

"You're crazy, Felicity. Completely *loco*. It doesn't make sense to go to all this trouble to own a horse you can't even ride."

"Perhaps," Felicity admitted with a shrug. "But it's no longer just a question of ownership."

"It's not?" Andi frowned. She must be tired. She had no idea what Felicity was talking about.

"No. It's the fact that no housemaid—no matter what your name is—will get the best of me." She took a deep breath. "The horse is mine, and your signature on this bill of sale will prove it. Sign it now and you'll save yourself a lot of trouble."

"No."

"Suit yourself," Felicity said. "You'll sign it sooner or later." She stood in the open doorway and regarded her prisoner. "I'll come back this afternoon to see if you've changed your mind. Here's breakfast." She took a canteen and a small gunnysack from Matt and tossed them at Andi's feet. "Be thinking about how long you'd like to stay in here."

"I'll never sign it," Andi declared in a tight voice. *"Never."*

"Yes, you will." Felicity smirked and closed the door with a loud *thud*. The shed was immediately cast into darkness.

Andi caught her breath and backed into a corner, all courage and brave words forgotten as true, gut-wrenching fear overwhelmed her.

"You talk real big, Andi Carter," she muttered, pulling her knees up against her chest to keep from shaking. "But that's all it is—*talk*."

She buried her head in her arms and let the tears come.

Andi heard the key turn in the lock and lurched to her feet. She braced herself for another confrontation with Felicity. For two full days and nights she had sat in this filthy shed and waited and waited and . . .

Stop it! Andi scolded herself. She wiped her eyes so Felicity could not see that she'd been crying again. There wasn't much to do in this dismal place but cry and pray, and Andi had been doing plenty of both.

She'd poured out her heart to God during those long, lonely hours when she was certain she would die of fear. She knew He'd heard her and even forgiven her for the foolish and wrong things she'd done lately. It came as a pleasant surprise, however, to actually feel less afraid after she prayed. The peace of knowing that God still loved her and was with her even in this dreary shed was a gift she wasn't about to forget.

Oh, Lord, she prayed when the door creaked open, *help me to be strong and make the right decision for once. I've made too many bad ones lately. What should I do about Taffy?*

Bright sunlight streamed into the shed, forcing Andi to blink and cover her eyes. Felicity entered, followed as usual by Matt.

"Ya know, Miss Felicity," Matt was grumbling, "I'm gettin' second thoughts. The boss ain't been too happy the past couple of days, thinkin' the girl's run off an' all. Now, with her family nosin' around, I—"

"Oh, hush," Felicity snapped. "You just keep thinking about all those waltzes I'm giving you next week at the spring dance." She reached into her sleeve and pulled out a perfumed handkerchief.

Waving the small square of white in front of her nose, she approached Andi and coughed. "Phew! How do you stand the smell in here? Another day of this and you won't be able to breathe." With her other hand, Felicity tossed another sack and canteen at Andi's feet.

Andi made no move to pick them up. She folded her arms across her chest and silently watched Felicity. She couldn't help noticing how fresh and clean the older girl appeared in her split skirt, vest, and bright blue blouse. A matching blue bow pulled back her curls.

In contrast, Andi knew she was filthy. The white blouse and color-ful skirt Nila had exchanged so many days ago for her overalls were gray with grime from living on the dirt floor. She had tried to keep her hands and face clean, but it proved impossible. The water from the canteen served only to turn the dust on her hands to mud. Now, in the light of a bright afternoon, she realized just how dreadful she must look.

Felicity smiled, as if reading Andi's mind. She held up the smudged, wrinkled bill of sale. "Ready to get out of this pigsty? Don't you want to go home?"

Home! Andi stared at the paper. *Yes, I want to go home, but—*

"What good does this do?" Matt complained from the doorway. He leaned against the doorpost and crossed his long, gangly arms over his chest. "She won't change her mind."

"She will today," Felicity replied without turning around. "Won't you, Andrea?"

Andi looked past Felicity into the freedom of a lovely afternoon. It would be so easy to sign the paper and walk away from this place.

Then she remembered the lash marks on her horse. She shook her head. She couldn't leave Taffy with Felicity.

A sly smile curled Felicity's lips. "I met your family today."

The words struck Andi like a slap in the face. She flinched. "You're lying."

"You don't believe me? It's one of the reasons I'm late coming to see you." She settled herself against the wall next to the open doorway and stared at the ceiling as if deep in thought. "Let's see if I can remember this correctly. Your mother has light hair, with just a little gray. She dresses nicely and carries herself like a lady. Your sister is golden-haired and real pretty. About my age, wouldn't you say?"

Andi held her breath at Felicity's words. Her mind spun. Her entire family was here on the Lazy L? It was incredible. How had they found her?

Felicity was still talking. "I wouldn't mind getting to know your brothers better. They're quite good-looking." She blushed. "The two older ones are dark-haired like you, but the younger brother is blond and so very friendly."

"He won't be friendly when he finds out what you did to me," Andi replied.

Mitch would probably want to shake the living daylights out of Felicity. And Chad? Well, Chad wasn't very good about turning the other cheek, especially if someone he loved had been hurt.

Andi pushed from her mind the image of her brothers handing out their own idea of justice. From Felicity's descriptions, she knew the girl spoke the truth about her family's arrival on the ranch. Hope soared. "How did they find me?"

"They *haven't* found you," Felicity reminded Andi with a laugh. "They're up at the house. You're tucked away here, where they'll never find you." She took a step toward the doorway then turned to face Andi. "They'll be leaving soon. Papa told them he didn't know where you were, which is the truth. He doesn't know. I suppose they'll look around a bit, ask folks in town, and head back to their fancy ranch up north." She sighed. "A pity, really. Your mother looked so tired and sad."

A lump came to Andi's throat. Her mother was here, looking for her. Her brothers—and even Melinda—had come, hoping to find her on the Lazy L. They must be worried sick. She'd been gone so long.

I'm getting out of here, she decided, swallowing hard. The lump in her throat disappeared. *My family's not going home without me. They've suffered enough on my account.*

Andi squared her shoulders and looked at the paper in Felicity's hand. With fresh insight, she realized she was not going to win this battle. Suddenly, it didn't matter if she won, or if Felicity won. What really mattered was going home so that her *family* could win. It was the right decision—the only decision.

She had to give Taffy up.

"I'll sign it," Andi said, clenching her jaw. With an ache in her heart that hurt worse than Felicity's whip, she held out her hand.

"It's about time." Smiling her triumph, Felicity took a filled pen from her pocket and thrust both it and the paper under Andi's nose.

Andi scrawled her name on the line. Just like that, she condemned her best friend to the mercy of Felicity Livingston. She choked back a sob and threw the pen and paper to the ground.

Felicity snatched up her precious document. Then she shoved Andi out the door. "You're free to go. I don't care where. But don't ever step foot on the Lazy L again." She pointed toward the faint outline of a little-used road leading west. "Town is that way. Start walking."

Andi brushed past Felicity.

"Oh, I almost forgot," Felicity called her back. She grabbed Andi's hand and slapped two shiny gold coins in her palm. "Here's your twenty dollars, just to keep things legal."

Andi flung the money at Felicity's feet. Then she turned and fled.

Chapter Seventeen

A LONG WALK

A ndi didn't know how far it was to town or what she would do when she got there. She only knew she was hot, sweaty, and dreadfully tired. She hoped she wasn't lost. The old wagon path Felicity had pointed out wound its way alongside gullies and through small creeks for what seemed like miles and miles. When it finally joined up with a road that looked well-traveled, Andi stopped to rest. A crooked sign with the words *Livingston Flats—3 mi.* and an arrow pointed the way to town.

"Three more miles!" Andi exclaimed, dismayed. She took a deep breath and slowly began the trek into town. As she trudged along the dusty road, she thought about what would happen when she reached Livingston Flats. Perhaps the sheriff would let her stay in his office. Maybe he'd give her something to eat.

She looked down at herself and shook her head. "Most likely he'll toss me into the horse trough first."

Andi sighed. Worse than seeing the sheriff was the thought of explaining Taffy's new owner to her family. *I never imagined it would end like this, not in my worst nightmare.*

How stubborn and foolish she'd been to cling to the hopeless task of finding Taffy on her own! She should have returned home the minute the Garduño family offered to take her, confessed how she'd lost Taffy, and asked for help. Her brothers would have done everything in their power to find the palomino.

I did everything wrong. Again. Even knowing she was forgiven didn't ease the sharp sting of leaving Taffy behind.

The minutes crawled by. Andi shaded her eyes, longing to see some sign of civilization. The town appeared as a smudge of dark shapes on the horizon. "This is the longest three miles of my life," she muttered.

Spotting a huge oak tree next to the road, Andi headed for it. She threw herself to the ground beneath its spreading branches. What a relief to be out from under the glaring sun! Mindful of her painful back, she stretched out on her belly and gazed down the road.

"If only a rider would come by," Andi wished aloud. "Or a wagon, or a . . . well, anything with wheels or hooves. I wouldn't be too proud to ask for a ride." She saw no one. Her eyelids began to flutter. "I'll just close my eyes for one minute . . ."

The sound of hoofbeats roused Andi from her dozing. She yawned and blinked against the brightness. Shading her eyes, she sat up and squinted toward the road. Her heart leaped. A horse and rider were galloping her way from the direction of the Livingston ranch.

Andi sprang to her feet, suddenly alert. *This is my chance to hitch a ride to town.* She cupped her hands to her mouth and shouted at the top of her lungs. "Hey, you! Whoever you are! Stop!"

In her excitement at discovering a potential ride, Andi completely forgot no one could hear her from so far away. She waved her arms over her head and took off running toward the horse. "Stop!" she hollered when the rider drew closer. She planted herself in the horse's path and held up her hands. *"Stop!"*

Andi's strategy to attract the rider's attention worked. He yanked back on the reins to avoid running her over. "Whoa, there!"

The horse came to an abrupt halt. Snorting and sidestepping, his stamping hooves churned up a cloud of dust.

Andi stumbled against the horse. He shied away, but she grasped the bridle. She couldn't let her only chance for a ride to town get away.

"Please, mister, I need a ride." Her eyes watered from the choking dust. She coughed and looked up into the rider's face. "Are you headed for—" She broke off with a gasp. "Chad?"

Chad's mouth fell open. *"Andi?"* With a slight pull on the reins, he steadied his horse and leaped from the saddle. He reached out to steady her. "Are you all right? Where have you been?"

Andi hesitated only a moment. Then she launched herself at her brother and threw her arms around his neck. "Oh, Chad!" she said, nearly choking him in her embrace. "You're here. You found me. I've been so scared."

"Hey, take it easy." Chad untangled her shaking arms from around his neck and lowered her to the ground. "You're safe now."

Andi rubbed her eyes. "How did you find me?"

Chad pulled a bandana from his back pocket and handed it over. "You're a mess." He grinned.

It was so like Chad to focus on the little things, like Andi's dirty face and filthy clothes, that she smiled back. "How did you—"

"It was Senator Farley." Chad nodded at Andi's astonishment. "He was passing through town on his way back to Sacramento and learned that you were still missing. He told Justin he'd seen a girl on Randall Livingston's ranch he at first thought was you, but then he figured he had to be mistaken when she only spoke Spanish. It was a long shot, but we'd searched everywhere else, so we decided to try the Lazy L."

Chad caught Andi up in another embrace and held her close. "I was so scared I'd never see you again," he whispered. "Some folks might say the senator crossing paths with you was a remarkable coincidence, but I prefer to believe it was God's grace arranging things."

Andi agreed. God had been good to her in spite of everything she'd done wrong. She slid out of Chad's arms, suddenly ashamed—ashamed that her brother looked so happy to see her. He should be angry, disgusted with her behavior.

"I'm so sorry," she apologized. Her throat tightened. "I would've come home that very night, except Taffy got stolen and I had to find her. It's all my fault, and I promise I'll never—"

"It's not entirely your fault," Chad broke in. "I'm to blame for some of it. We didn't realize until too late that you'd overheard our discussion. I should have kept my big mouth shut. I sometimes forget that you're not quite twelve years old. Justin is right. I need more patience."

He let out a long, tired sigh. "But thank God it's over now and you're safe."

"No, Chad. It's not over. It's worse than you could ever guess. I lost Taffy. I tried to keep her, but—"

"I know. You told me. But she can't be far. We'll find her." He mounted his horse and reached out a hand to pull her up. "Let's go."

"You don't understand," Andi insisted as she settled herself behind her brother. "I know where Taffy is. She's on the Livingston ranch. "But"—she swallowed and tightened her hold around Chad's waist— "she doesn't belong to me anymore. I . . . I gave her to Felicity."

"You *what?*" Chad barked. Then he softened his voice. "Maybe you'd better tell me the whole story." He urged the horse forward. "We've got a ways to go."

In a rush of words, Andi poured out the events of the past three weeks—the drifter who stole Taffy, the kindness of the Garduño family, and her futile attempts to locate Taffy in the towns they passed through. She explained how she'd come to the Lazy L and what she'd done there as a servant. She omitted nothing, not even her plan to save Felicity's horse by stealing it.

"The horse turned out to be Taffy," she said. "I guess I went sort of crazy when I saw Felicity hitting her. I didn't think. I just rushed in and tried to stop her." She took a deep breath and told the rest of her story in a hurry. Felicity's cruelty was not something she wanted to dwell on.

"And so I signed the paper," Andi finished sorrowfully. "I had no choice, not when I heard you'd all come to the Lazy L looking for me."

"You were backed into a corner, all right," Chad agreed. "You made the right choice."

"But I lost Taffy. Can you—" Andi gulped back the tears that threatened to spill. "Can you ever forgive me for that?"

Chad brought his horse to a stop. He shifted around and looked at Andi. His eyes held no accusation. No annoyance. Only compassion. "Forgiving you is the easy part, little sister. The hard part will be learning to live with what's happened."

He laid a gentle hand on Andi's head. "I'm sorry about Taffy. It hurts to lose something you love, and the pain doesn't go away. But you need to know we would sacrifice Taffy in an instant to get you back. If you'd figured that out a couple of weeks ago, you could have saved yourself a lot of grief—and the rest of us too." He turned around and urged Sky into a lope.

Andi laid her head against her brother's strong back and squeezed her eyes shut to keep the tears from flowing. Chad was right. She'd have to live with what she'd done. It was a punishment worse than any her mother could think up. Going to the barn each morning and finding an empty stall would be a continual reminder of how foolish she'd been. She didn't know if she could bear it.

But she had to. She'd made her choice.

C

Although Andi rode behind her brother in perfect safety, she couldn't help shuddering when she caught sight of the Lazy L ranch house. It rose before her like a bad dream when they loped up the broad, shady lane and into the yard. She tightened her hold around

Chad's waist and whispered, "Felicity told me never to come back here."

"Don't worry," Chad assured her. "You're with me. She can't hurt you ever again." He slowed the horse to a trot and called out in his typical, exuberant manner, "Mother! Where are you? Justin? I'm back!"

He pulled Sky up next to the hitching post and lowered Andi to the ground. "Where is everybody?" He dismounted and carelessly wrapped the reins around the post.

The door to the Livingston home opened. Randall Livingston strode onto the veranda, followed by Andi's mother, sister, and two brothers.

"Chad!" Elizabeth hurried along the brick walkway. "You're back from town already? What did you learn from the sheriff about—"

"Mother!" Andi shouted.

"Andrea?" Her mother's voice was an astonished whisper.

Andi pushed past Chad, raced up the walkway, and threw herself into her mother's welcoming embrace. Looking up into her face, she saw lines of worry and fear etched across her features. *She's all worn out because of me.* "I'm *so* sorry, Mother."

Elizabeth nodded wordlessly and held Andi close. She looked up as Chad approached. "How did you find her?"

"Apparently, she's been in a shed about five or six miles east of here." Chad's expression hardened. "Kept there until she agreed to sign over Taffy to Livingston's daughter. I met up with her on the road to town. Quite a walk for a young girl." He eyed the Lazy L rancher. "You've got a lot of explaining to do, mister."

An uneasy expression filled Mr. Livingston's face. "The girl disappeared a couple of days ago, but I thought she'd run off. I assure you, I had no idea she was still on my ranch. Had I known, I would have certainly intervened."

Chad clenched his fists and took a step toward the man. His eyes flashed. "I suppose you know nothing about my sister's whipping, either."

In the heavy silence that followed, Andi could hear the rustling of trees and the quiet swishing of a horse's tail. She felt her mother's arms tighten around her and heard the quick intake of her breath. From the corner of her eye she saw Felicity lower herself onto the porch swing and clasp her fingers together in her lap. Standing beside her, Mrs. Nelson was watching everything. A thoughtful frown creased her forehead.

Mr. Livingston broke the silence with a deep sigh. "An unfortunate accident. I apologize." He smiled at Andi's mother. "You know how quickly these things can get blown out of proportion, Mrs. Carter. It was nothing more than a misunderstanding between the girls over a horse. It's all settled now, isn't it, Felicity?"

"Indeed it is, Papa."

He turned back to Elizabeth. "You see? It's over. I hope you'll accept my sincere apologies and let the matter go."

Andi knew better than to interrupt her elders, but she could hardly contain herself. She wanted to leap at Mr. Livingston and make him tell the truth.

Chad saved her from doing anything so reckless. "Sure, Livingston," he offered generously. "We'll forget the whole thing. Just return my sister's horse, and we'll be on our way."

Andi's heart swelled with love for Chad. Dizzy with hope, she straightened up to listen.

"I'm afraid that will be impossible," Mr. Livingston said. He motioned to Felicity, who rose and came to stand beside her father. "My daughter has a signed bill of sale for the horse. She told me she got it the day before your sister disappeared."

That's a lie! Andi opened her mouth to voice her outrage, but Mother's firm pressure on her arm silenced her.

Mr. Livingston took the soiled bill of sale from Felicity. From his pocket he pulled out another slip of paper. He waved both in

Chad's face. "I bought the mare in good faith from Jon March." He grunted. "Cost me a pretty penny too. Felicity offered Andrea twenty dollars. It's all right here."

Chad snatched the papers from the rancher's hand and scanned them. Then he passed them to Justin, who stood quietly off to one side, watching the exchange. "You're the lawyer, Justin. These look legal to you?"

Justin skimmed the documents. "They appear to be." He glanced up at Mr. Livingston, who was nodding in satisfaction. "Except for one or two small details."

"What's that?" the man snapped.

"My sister is not of age. Her signature means nothing without mine." Justin shot the rancher an accusing glance. "As I'm sure you were already aware."

He handed back the worthless papers. "The bill of sale from the livery stable isn't worth the paper it's written on. It's for stolen property. No more games, Mr. Livingston. Admit you made a mistake. We'll give you what you paid for the mare. In addition, we'll cover the cost of her board while she was in your care."

"No, Papa." Felicity stamped her foot. "She's mine."

Justin ignored the outburst. "It's a fair offer. Our brand is on the horse, and you can't produce a legitimate bill of sale. That could cause you difficulties in a court of law."

Mr. Livingston chewed his lip, looking thoughtful. Finally, he spoke. "I'm sorry, Felicity. The horse is not worth the trouble these folks can give me."

"You're *not* sorry!" Felicity shrieked.

Her father did not reply. Instead, he beckoned to a ranch hand. "Go to the barn and bring out the palomino. I've had enough of this."

"Sure thing, boss." He strode away.

Andi watched with a pounding heart. The worst was over, she was sure. Her big brothers had achieved in five minutes what all her suffering and hard work had failed to accomplish during the past three weeks: getting Taffy back. She caught Justin looking at her and grinned her thanks.

He winked.

"Hey, boss!" the ranch hand emerged from the barn, shouting. "The stall's empty. The palomino's gone."

Chapter Eighteen

END OF THE RIDE

Gone? Icy fingers squeezed Andi's heart. She flicked a startled look at Felicity and caught her smiling slyly. *She knows where Taffy is!*

Andi wanted to hit the wretched girl. Then she remembered—she'd made her choice. She'd given Taffy up so she could go home. Getting her horse back had been an unexpected miracle. Now it appeared that Felicity would win, after all.

Andi didn't know if she could lose Taffy a second time. She took a deep, shaky breath. *Help me, God*, she pleaded silently. *I can't do this alone.*

"This has gone far enough." Mrs. Nelson's voice crackled with irritation. She marched across the porch and planted herself in front of her employer. Her gray eyes snapped. "I'm ashamed that Felicity has been allowed to act like this. I've overlooked many of her actions in the past out of loyalty to this family. But *this*? It's not decent. I won't stand for it."

She drew herself up. "You may dismiss me if you like, sir, but I will be silent no longer. You must do something about your daughter's behavior before it's too late."

"Mrs. Nelson!" Mr. Livingston exclaimed. "You forget yourself."

The housekeeper set her jaw. "I will finish what I have to say. Then if you wish, I will pack my bags and leave." She drew a deep breath.

"Sir, you imagine Felicity as a heartbroken little girl still mourning her mother's death. You comforted her then by giving in to her every whim. It's become a dangerous habit. I've expressed my concerns many times in the past, but you brushed them aside like so many discarded rags." She drew a handkerchief from her apron pocket and wiped her eyes.

Andi watched in bewilderment. Mrs. Nelson *crying*? Over *Felicity*? It was incredible.

The housekeeper sniffed back her tears. "Felicity is no longer a child. She's nearly a grown woman and has not yet learned self-control or consideration for others. I love her, Mr. Livingston, and I was afraid. She was so set on keeping that horse, to the point of acting irrationally." She stared at her employer with haunted eyes. "The Carter girl was *locked in a shed*. What if Felicity had been prevented from going out there? Andrea could have met her death. What then, sir?"

Mr. Livingston paled. It was obvious his housekeeper's words were affecting him, causing him to grasp—perhaps for the first time—the enormity of his daughter's crimes. He turned a piercing gaze on Felicity. "Where's the palomino?"

Felicity shrugged, stone-faced.

"I saw Matt leading the mare toward town not too long after you folks arrived," Mrs. Nelson supplied, tilting her head toward Elizabeth.

Mr. Livingston nodded. "Then she's at the livery." He bowed slightly to Andi's mother. "I'll saddle my horse and accompany you into town. Jon will be more willing to hand over the mare if I'm along. Besides," he added, grim-faced, "I believe he and I have a little matter of a stolen horse to discuss."

"Papa?" Felicity asked. "What about *me*?"

Mr. Livingston regarded his daughter coldly. "You have shamed me today, Felicity," he said in a voice that made Andi's eyes open wide in astonishment. "All because of your obsession over a horse. Mrs. Nelson is right. I've been blind to your faults for too long. Now my eyes are open. There will be some changes." He drew in a long, ragged breath. "I only pray for all our sakes that it is not too late."

Felicity's face went white at her father's words. She clasped her hands tightly and blinked back tears. "Papa," she whispered. "What are you saying? How can you—"

"Enough." There was no hint of gentleness in the rancher's voice. "Go to your room. I will deal with you when I return."

Felicity fled indoors, sobbing. With a smile and a nod of approval at Mr. Livingston, Mrs. Nelson turned and followed her young mistress into the house.

"So, what are we all standing around for?" Mitch's cheerful voice jerked Andi's attention from where she stood, staring after Felicity's retreating form. He picked her up and gave her a hug. "Let's get Taffy and go home."

Once Andi was safely home, she didn't care what kind of discipline she received. She welcomed the chance to show her family how much she appreciated their sacrifice. Her brothers had left the ranch in their foreman's hands to search the countryside for her during spring roundup, the busiest time of the year. It made Andi feel a little like the lost sheep in the parable Jesus told.

"This is one sheep who doesn't intend to ever get lost again," she assured Taffy a few days later. She looked up and sighed. "That's a promise, Lord. You took care of me when I acted so foolishly, and You brought me home." She threw her arms around her horse's neck and hugged her tight. "You even gave me Taffy back. Thank You for loving and forgiving me when I didn't deserve it."

With a grateful smile, Andi ran her hand over the healing cuts on her mare's neck. Chad had done a splendid job tending Taffy. He promised she'd be as good as new in a couple of weeks. Andi's own injuries had already faded to a minor annoyance.

She reached for a brush. "Two weeks should be just about right." She'd been forbidden to ride for two weeks as part of her punishment. The other part included a list of chores a mile long. She'd be too busy to go anywhere but school for ages. "Which is fine by me, girl. We've had our fill of adventure, haven't we?"

Taffy nickered her agreement and nibbled Andi's hair.

"*Señorita, ¿dónde estás?*"

"I'm in here, Diego," she called to the ranch hand.

Diego made his way to Taffy's stall and leaned over the half-door. "The *señora* wishes you to come up to the house. You have visitors."

"Visitors?" Andi frowned and dropped the brush into the grooming box. "Who are they?"

Diego shook his head and shrugged. "*No sé.*"

Andi left Taffy's stall and followed Diego out of the barn. With a wave of thanks, she sprinted around the side of the ranch house and up the front porch. Who could be visiting her today?

She flung open the door, walked into the wide foyer, and stopped short. The Garduño family stood beside Andi's mother, looking uncomfortable and out of place.

"*¡Señor! ¡Señora! ¡Qué sorpresa!*" The biggest surprise of Andi's life. "What are you doing here?"

"We came to tell your family where to find you," Nila explained. "But your mother told us you were already home, *gracias a Dios.*"

"Yes," José added with a smile. "My wife fussed and worried so much about leaving you on the Lazy L, I decided we could not let the *ranchero* frighten us with his warnings to keep silent."

Andi grasped Nila by the hand. "I'm so glad you're here." She looked at her mother. "This is the family I told you about, Mother. The ones who took care of me."

Elizabeth nodded. "Yes. We were getting acquainted while we waited for you." She turned to José and Nila. "I'm grateful to you for looking after Andrea these past few weeks. She told me how you wanted to bring her home, but she wouldn't cooperate. How can we repay your kindness?"

José held up his hand. "Please, *señora*, it was our good fortune to find your daughter. She repaid us many times during her stay."

"There must be something we could do to show our gratitude."

"There is nothing," José insisted. He motioned to Nila. "The child is safe. We must be going." He paused. "I do have one question, *señora*. We are unfamiliar with this part of the valley. Do you know of any steady work nearby?"

"Indeed I do," Elizabeth answered without hesitation. "There's work right here for your entire family. Luisa's getting on in years and would welcome your wife's help with the meals and housework."

She smiled at José. "Our foreman can't seem to keep a full crew to cover all the jobs around here during the spring and summer. He'll find plenty of work for you and your son."

"Gracias, señora." José bowed respectfully. "It would be an honor to work for you and your fine family."

Andi threw her arms around Rosa. "You get to stay! I know just where you can live. It's a little cabin a mile or so past the house. It will be so nice having a girl my age on the ranch. I'll teach you more English so you can go to school with me in the fall and—"

"Chiquita," Nila interrupted. "Rosa will be working. She will not have much time for anything else."

Andi grinned. "We'll see." She turned to Joselito. "And you, Joselito. Maybe you'll become a cowboy, after all."

The boy beamed. "I would like that very much."

"Mother?" Andi asked. "While you're settling everyone, may I take Rosa and Joselito to see Taffy?"

Elizabeth smiled. "Of course."

"Taffy's right out back," Andi told her friends. "Come on. I'll show you." She grabbed Rosa's hand and headed for the door. "When we're in the barn, you'll have to see all the stalls I've mucked out since I got home."

She made a face. "Chad saved them for me. Every last one of them." She laughed. "Actually, it's not such a bad job. I've had worse."

Andi met Rosa's look of understanding and squeezed her hand. It was so good to be home!

A literature unit study guide with enrichment activities is available for *Andrea Carter and the Long Ride Home* as a free download at www.CircleCAdventures.com.

Contact Susan K. Marlow at susankmarlow@kregel.com

FOLLOW JEM AND HIS SISTER, ELLIE!

Twelve-year-old Jem stumbles into exciting adventures in the Goldtown Adventures series

Badge of Honor • Tunnel of Gold
Canyon of Danger • River of Peril

Check out Jem's Web site at
www.goldtownadventures.com

Grow Up with Andi!

**Don't miss any of Andi's adventures in the
Circle C Beginnings series**

Andi's Pony Trouble
Andi's Indian Summer
Andi's Fair Surprise
Andi's Scary School Days
Andi's Lonely Little Foal
Andi's Circle C Christmas

And you can visit www.AndiandTaffy.com
for free coloring pages, learning activities, puzzles
you can do online, and more!